BOUND BY MAGIC

MAGIC AWAKENED #1

SADIE MOSS

For More Information:
www.SadieMossAuthor.com

For updates on new releases, promotions, and giveaways, sign up for my
MAILING LIST.

CHAPTER 1

THE MAN in the blue tunic opened his mouth and let out a high-pitched scream.

Or at least, that's what it sounded like to me. I'd been told that, among the more refined classes, what he was doing was considered singing, but my eardrums begged to differ—thank you very much. It didn't help that I couldn't understand a word he was saying, though I was pretty sure he was technically speaking English.

I surveyed the audience from the shadows, wondering if any of them actually enjoyed opera, or if they just didn't want to be the first in their social circle to admit they hated it.

Who would actually pay good money to subject themselves to this?

Apparently, over a thousand members of the magical elite of Denver, that's who.

The theatre was enormous, with a large ground-level seating area and three balcony levels rising above it. I lingered

1

in the shadows at the back of the third balcony. The season ticket holders in this section must have decided they wanted to preserve their hearing a little longer, because this area was much more sparsely filled than the main floor. Perfect.

The man onstage opened his mouth again, nearly unhinging his jaw to release a single sustained note. I grimaced, resisting the urge to stick my fingers in my ears.

Badass mercenary Lana Crow will not be brought down by an opera singer, damn it.

Still, I pulled my dark wool cap lower on my head, covering my ears a bit more. I told myself I wasn't doing it to block out the sound, but simply to make sure none of my flame-red hair peeked out and drew unwanted attention to me.

After glowering at the man in the blue tunic for a moment longer, I shifted my focus away.

I wasn't here for him, after all.

Nope, that dubious honor belonged to the man sitting in the seat four rows ahead of me.

Gerald Marceau.

He was the reason I was pressed against the wall at the back of the balcony, dressed head-to-toe in black like a rogue stagehand. I didn't know much about Gerald aside from his name and the fact that I was supposed to deliver him alive to collect my bounty. Oh, and he was Gifted, which meant he had some sort of magical ability. I could feel the power coming off him from where I stood, but unfortunately it didn't give me any clue as to what he could actually *do*.

Some Gifted felt incredibly powerful—until you realized

their only power was creating potions that turned into five course meals or something. A kitchen witch might become the world's best magical "chef," but that hardly made her a threat. However, other Gifted people held massive amounts of magic at their fingertips and weren't limited to one kind of spell casting. Powerful mages could learn new kinds of magic with intense study and dedication, and most of it would do a lot worse than give you a stomachache.

Sadly, in the social strata, I ranked far below both the kitchen witch and the mage. I was one of the Blighted, with no magic at my command. That lack of magic didn't leave me completely powerless though, something the Gifted seemed to forget all too often.

Oh well. Made my job easier, really. They never saw the threat coming. Not from little ol' Blighted me.

Speaking of which....

The man in the blue tunic had been joined by a whole cadre of similarly dressed people onstage, and as the music swelled to deafening levels, I crept forward. My feet didn't make a sound, though it hardly mattered with the racket going on in here.

If I didn't make this catch now, I'd lose my chance. I'd been following Gerald for hours, and I had seen the heavy wards and enchantments that protected his house. If he made it home safe tonight, he'd stay that way. There was no way I'd be able to break through those wards.

A public grab was never ideal, but with a midnight deadline on his delivery, I was running out of options.

Gerald was a popular guy. This was the first time all day

he'd been even semi-alone. The only potential witnesses present now were the few other audience members scattered in the rows ahead of him and the petite blonde woman next to him. The blonde might be a problem though. She was draped around him so tight it was like she was auditioning for the role of "pashmina." I wondered if he'd had to pay for her seat, considering she wasn't really using it.

Dammit, why did Gerald's date have to be so fucking *friendly?* They were practically glued together.

First order of business, extract Gerald from Blondie's clutches. Second order of business, subdue him and get him out of here. And do it all before the final curtain falls.

No problem.

I walked quietly down the steps toward Gerald's seat as the cacophony below continued unabated. I wasn't even sure the singers had taken a breath yet. Maybe they were using magic. When I reached the large man, I tapped him lightly on the shoulder. Gerald had been watching the opera raptly—did he actually *like* it?—but he flinched when I touched him and looked up sharply.

"Excuse me, sir," I whispered. "I'm sorry to disturb you, but you have an urgent message from Leo Barrett."

I'd overheard Gerald screaming into his cell phone at someone by that name several times today, so I figured there was a good chance it would get his attention. Sure enough, he grunted and pried the blonde's grasping fingers away from him to stand up.

"For fuck's sake. I knew it! What'd he do now?"

I ducked my head solicitously. "If you'll just come with me,

4

sir."

"I'll just be a minute, baby." He shushed the blonde's whispered protests and followed me up the aisle to the door at the back.

Holding it open for him, I allowed him to step through ahead of me, pointing down the hallway. "It's that way, sir."

Grumbling, Gerald ambled down the dimly lit hall. I pulled the door shut behind us as I quickly drew a pair of iridescent black handcuffs from my back pocket. They glowed slightly in the dark, giving away their magical enhancement. Hey, I wasn't above using a few charms or enchanted objects to even the playing field a bit.

Stepping close to Gerald, I reached for his thick wrist, but froze when the door behind us banged open again and a high-pitched voice called out.

"Gerald, baby, come back! You're missing the best part. I— Hey, what are you doing?"

The blonde noticed the handcuffs at the same moment Gerald spun around, his eyes widening. *Shit.* I dove for his wrist, but before I could slip the cuffs on, he raised his hand, fingers splayed. A burst of ice shot from his palm, slamming into me and throwing me backward. I flew past the blonde and skidded on the plush carpet. Coughing, I worked to pull air into my lungs as I crouched on all fours. That blast of ice had hurt like a bitch.

So that's what he can do. Great.

Blondie's wide eyes darted between me and Gerald for a second, and then her mouth dropped open just like the opera singer's had.

Oh, fuck no.

Scrambling to my feet, I nailed her with a punch just as the first high note of her scream pierced the air. She staggered back and crumpled to the ground, blood pouring from her nose. By the time I turned around, Gerald was already dashing down the hall. He was a big guy, both in height and girth, but he moved fast.

I spared a quick glance at his abandoned date. Her head was propped against the wall, her mouth hanging open slightly and her eyes half-closed. Gerald didn't even look back as he rounded the stairwell leading down to the main floor.

Wow, what a gentleman.

My lip curled in disgust as I raced after him. I shouldn't be surprised one of the Gifted was putting his own self-interest before anybody else's. It was a hallmark of their kind.

As I darted into the stairwell, I shoved the handcuffs back in my pocket. I'd need them once I caught up to him.

Our footsteps slapped in a discordant beat on the steps, his almost a full floor below mine, though he was losing some of his lead already. He hit the last step running, and I picked up my pace. A startled looking usher dressed all in black jerked out of the way as I barreled past him. It wasn't like he could do much to stop me though. He had the same amount of magic I did—none.

It wasn't surprising to see another Blighted in the Capital. The Gifted needed people to cater their parties, usher their operas, cook for them, clean for them, and drive them around, so they allowed us into the Capital to work. We just weren't allowed to live here.

Well, mostly. I had heard rumors of a few Blighted citizens wealthy enough to buy their way into high society, smothering themselves with magical charms, spells, and enchantments in an attempt to blend in. But I'd never actually met one, and I wasn't sure I believed the stories. Why would anyone do that? If I had that kind of money, I wouldn't waste it trying to pass as Gifted. I'd buy myself a private island a million miles away from here.

The short, skinny guy muttered a half-hearted rebuke, then slunk away. It was possible he was going to tell his superiors about the disturbance, but I doubted it. As one of the Blighted, he was as likely to be punished as praised for sticking his nose into a Gifted man's business. Most Blighted, especially those who worked in the Capital, learned to keep their heads down and their mouths shut.

Gerald yanked open one of the grand entrance doors at the front of the building and dashed out into the night. I barely caught the edge of the door before it closed, hauling it back open and slipping out after him. My eyes tracked left and right, catching sight of his absurd tuxedo tails flapping in the breeze as he ran down 14th Street.

Fucking Blondie. She couldn't have survived without him for one godsdamned minute?

I swore under my breath as I sprinted after him. If I didn't deliver him unconscious and in one piece by midnight, I wouldn't get paid.

That thought was enough to give my pace a boost, and I gained a few yards on the large man in front of me. We were in the theatre district, and the evening's performances hadn't let out yet, so there were only a few people on the streets. But it only took one to call the Peacekeepers—the magical law enforcement. I needed to end this now and get out of here quick.

A small park opened up on the left, and Gerald darted into it, weaving around a few perfectly manicured trees. He twisted slightly, looking behind him as he shot another blast of ice at me. I dodged left.

Because I was facing forward and Gerald was facing backward, I saw what he didn't. His route was about to be abruptly cut off by Cherry Creek.

It'd been given that name a long time ago, but the description no longer fit. Sometime in the last decade, the Denver city planners had decided instead of a muddy brown, meandering stream, a wide, clear blue river would be a more aesthetically pleasing accent to the Capital. The broad expanse of water was contained by stone walls on either side, and a pathway lit by old-fashioned streetlamps wended along Cherry Creek's edge, several feet above the rushing water below.

Gerald's arms pinwheeled as he tried to change direction fast enough to avoid plunging into the river. His feet went out from under him, and he slid sideways.

Ah ha!

Pumping my arms furiously in a final burst of speed, I threw myself at the big man, hitting him in a full-body tackle as he struggled to rise. He went down like a felled tree, cushioning my fall by landing beneath me.

"Hold still, you asshole," I muttered, trying to keep him

pinned with my body while I scrabbled in my back pocket for the charmed handcuffs again. If I could get them on him, this fight would end real quick.

The guy weighed twice as much as I did, but he obviously didn't have much experience with fighting—he likely solved most of his problems with magic. I was able to outmaneuver him, pinning his arms above his head so he couldn't blast me again while he bucked and thrashed. Our position probably looked extremely indecent.

Unfortunately, with both hands occupied restraining Gerald, it was damn hard to get the cuffs on him. They were caught in my right hand, pressed to the skin of his wrist as I bore down with all my weight. Too bad the sedation charm would only take effect once the things were actually on him.

Gerald panted and cursed, his puffy cheeks blotchy and a sheen of sweat covering his brow.

Scooting up higher so I was sitting on his chest, I pinned his upper arms with my knees to free my hands, then grabbed for his wrist again.

Just as the cuff was about to clamp onto his wrist, Gerald howled and yanked his arm free, a flurry of icicles flying from his fingertips. I turned my head to avoid getting stabbed in the eye, and my knee slammed into the pavement as the handcuffs were ripped from my grasp.

In what seemed like slow motion, I watched them tumble through the air end over end... until they landed with a faint *plop* in the clear blue water of Cherry Creek.

CHAPTER 2

As my charmed handcuffs were carried away by the rushing water, Gerald took advantage of my momentary heartbreak to shove me off, sending another block of blue ice at me. It hit my chest hard. He clambered to his feet and took off down the river walk, his pace slower than it had been before. I couldn't blame him. I was feeling a little beat up myself. My ribs hurt like hell, making breathing difficult.

And I had no more magical cuffs.

Well, fuck. Guess I'm gonna have to do this the old-fashioned way.

Ignoring the aches in my body, I sprinted after Gerald, catching up with him as he rounded a bend in the river. Pulling up alongside him, I aimed a vicious kick at the back of his knee. His stride broke, his leg crumpling beneath him like a piece of straw. He went down with a yowl of pain.

I didn't let him get up.

Cocking my fist, I threw a punch at the back of his head, dropping all my weight into it.

Gerald collapsed with a grunt, his big body going limp.

Crouching next to him, I tried to get my breath back. I had to take tiny sips of air or pain shot through my ribs.

Bruised, I was pretty sure. Not broken.

"Shouldn't have blasted my damn cuffs into the river, Gerald," I muttered to his prone form. "You could be high as a kite right now instead of out cold."

The cuffs had a small dial on them I could use to adjust the level of sedation they imparted to the person wearing them. That came in very handy on collection jobs, especially when my target was a giant man like Gerald. Instead of having to haul an unconscious body around, I could just dope him up to the point of extreme docility and he'd walk—well, stumble—wherever I directed him.

A rabbit punch wasn't my preferred way of taking down a mark. Not because I felt bad for hitting him, but because it made the rest of my job so much harder.

Case in point: my car was at least a mile away, and Gerald's body in front of me resembled a miniature beached whale. Or at least, what I assumed one would look like. I'd never seen the ocean, although visiting it was at the top of my bucket list.

I stood up slowly, glancing around to make sure no late night strollers were passing by. The river walk was deserted, light pooling in warm halos around the streetlamps in between darker stretches. We weren't directly under a lamppost, so that was good.

I toed Gerald's body, and he rolled slightly before collapsing back into a limp mound of flesh.

Shit.

He had to have almost a hundred pounds on me. There was no way I could carry him all the way to my car. Not without drawing attention.

Heaving a sigh—then wincing in pain—I slipped a glass cylinder from my front pocket. It was just a bit smaller than a lipstick tube and was filled with a swirling purple smoke. I set it upright on the ground beside me, then bent to lift Gerald under the arms. Once I got him semi-upright, I stomped my foot down hard on the glass vial beside us. The smoke billowed out in a cloud, encompassing us both.

A moment later, it cleared, revealing a dark side street and my beat-up green Honda Accord. The car was an absolute piece of shit, and it looked even worse compared to the fancy vehicles around it. The paint was sun-bleached and blistered, the front passenger door was dented so badly it barely opened anymore, and the plastic over the back brake lights had been replaced with red tape.

I unlocked it and hefted Gerald into the back seat, grunting as I shoved his large body inside.

This job had turned into a shit show. No two ways about it.

That transport spell had been for emergencies only, and even though this did kind of count as an emergency, I never liked to use my charms and spelled gadgets if I could help it. That shit wasn't cheap.

So far tonight, I was out one pair of magical handcuffs and

one transport spell. The bounty for Gerald wouldn't even cover replacing those.

I finally wrestled the Gifted man's feet into the car and slammed the door, leaving his body awkwardly bunched up on my back seat. I hopped in behind the wheel and drove away, careful to stick to the speed limit. My shitty car was like a magnet for the Peacekeepers. They could always find some reason to give me a ticket.

Navigating my way through the Capital, I made sure to avoid River North, where the younger Gifted set would be partying until the sun rose. I kept to less busy streets, passing through neighborhoods filled with beautiful, ornate mansions. The People's Palace rose up to my right, its white walls lit with a magical glow even at this hour.

When I reached the wall that separated the Capital from the Outskirts, I breathed a sigh of relief as I passed through. The contrast between the two sides of the wall was stark. Here, rundown houses and apartment complexes lined the potholed, neglected streets. It was hard to tell sometimes which buildings were occupied and which weren't. Everything was dirty and dingy, and there were so few working streetlights left that the road was mostly cast in darkness.

But it was home.

I was also less likely to get pulled over or harassed by Peacekeepers here. The Gifted didn't bother trying to police the Outskirts, beyond going after any Blighted rabble-rousers who caused trouble for the elite. But crime among the Blighted population? The Gifted couldn't care less.

Adjusting my rearview mirror, I checked to make sure Gerald was still sleeping as I pulled my car into a large abandoned warehouse to the north of the city.

The warehouse was pitch black, so I left my headlights on, my body making the beams flicker as I crossed to the other side to haul Gerald out by his feet. After he was situated on the dirty floor of the warehouse, I yanked off my gloves and cap and tossed them on the seat, letting my red hair spill down over my shoulders.

My headlights flickered again, and I tensed, looking toward the back of the warehouse.

"Rat?" I called into the darkness, my hands curling into loose fists.

"Yeah, doll, it's me." The scrawny young man crossed back into the beam of my headlights as he walked toward me, squinting against the glare of the beams. "You got him?"

"Yup, he's right here. You got the money?"

"Sure I do, sweetheart. You know I always do."

I rolled my eyes. Rat liked to pretend he was the hero in some noir detective novel, not just a down-on-his-luck kid who'd fallen into a job as a liaison between unsavory types like me and the even less savory types who wanted to hire us. He couldn't have been older than eighteen, with a bulbous nose, big ears, and beady eyes. It was easy to see where his nickname came from.

Coming around the side of the car, Rat popped the collar of his trench coat as he peered at me through the darkness. "Rough night? You look like shit."

14

"It's rude to tell a lady she looks like shit, Rat." I cocked an eyebrow at him.

He chortled, the sound swallowed immediately by the huge empty space. "If I see any ladies, I'll be sure to remember that."

"All right, wise guy. Come on, pay up." I held out my hand, and he slapped a stack of bills into it. I made him wait while I counted it. He'd never shorted me before, but I knew better than to trust anybody I dealt with.

When I was satisfied the full payment was there, I shoved the money in my pocket and jerked my head toward Gerald's body. He moaned slightly, which meant he'd probably wake up soon. I wanted to get out of here before that became my problem.

I started to circle around to the driver's side of my car, when Rat called out to me. "Hey! You free tomorrow?"

Pausing with my hand on the door, I looked over the hood at him suspiciously. "Maybe. Why?"

"Relax, I'm not looking for a date. I got a job for you, is all. Good pay."

I pursed my lips. My ribs felt a bit better, but as that pain faded, the throbbing in my knee increased. I'd slammed my kneecap into the ground hard enough to leave a massive bruise. I didn't really want to do another job tomorrow night, especially if it went as badly as this one. Which, if I went in injured, it very well could. Besides...

"Yeah, I don't think so, Rat. Tomorrow's my birthday. I was planning on taking the day off—you know, to pamper myself."

Rat laughed again. "I don't even want to ask what a *lady*

like you considers pampering." He exaggerated the word "lady," and I considered throwing something at his head. He clucked his tongue. "No worries if you don't want it. Just thought I'd give you first crack at it, since it pays so well."

I blew out a breath. I knew exactly what he was doing, but I still couldn't stop myself from asking, "How much?"

"Five grand."

I almost choked. The job I'd just done had paid me five *hundred*. With five grand, I might finally have enough money in the little nest egg I was building to get out of this city.

Trying to keep my tone disinterested, I tilted my head. "What's the job?"

"Assassination. An incubus named Akio Sun. You ever heard of him?"

I shook my head. "No. Should I have?"

"Eh, probably not. If you were a lonely Gifted housewife, maybe. He's apparently been making his way through that crowd, doing what incubi do best."

"Ah. Right."

I tapped my fingers on the hood of my car thoughtfully. The assassination request made sense then. Probably some angry husband who'd caught his wife in bed with the incubus. Demons were part of the Touched class, like shifters, fairies, and pixies; they were magical beings, but couldn't wield magic like the Gifted could. They were treated better than the Blighted were, given voting rights and allowed to live and work in the Capital.

An assassination, though. Could I do that?

It was probably hypocritical to have an attack of

conscience about killing someone, when I was pretty sure a lot of the targets I brought in ended up meeting that same fate. But I wasn't the one doing the killing in those cases, and somehow that made a difference.

I bit my lip. Did the Touched really deserve my mercy? A lot of them treated us worse than the Gifted did, as if keeping us down somehow raised them up.

With a decisive nod, I turned to Rat. "Yeah. I'll do it."

"Perfect!" The gangly teen clapped his hands together and scurried around the front of the car. When he reached my side, he dug into the pocket of his trench coat and withdrew a small slip of paper. "All I have for you is the address. You'll have to do all the other legwork yourself. If you can make it look like an accident, that's ideal, but if you can't, just make it look like a robbery gone wrong or something."

Rat slapped the paper into my palm. His bony fingers were ice cold, sending a shiver racing up my arm. He probably hadn't had a full meal in weeks. A lot of people in the Outskirts were malnourished.

I squinted at the writing but couldn't make it out in the dark. I'd look up the address later. "Got it. Midnight deadline again?"

"Yep. Call me when it's done and I'll meet you with the money."

"All right. Take care of yourself, Rat."

"Yeah, you too, doll." He saluted me with two thin fingers as I slid into my car.

I cranked the key, and the engine turned over for a few seconds before rumbling to life. As I backed out of the warehouse, the headlights illuminated Rat struggling to lift Gerald. When he'd gotten the large man into a seated position, he stepped on the transport spell next to them. Purple smoke billowed out, and they vanished.

Pulling out onto the desolate road, I stuffed the piece of paper into the empty cup holder beside me.

Five. Thousand. Dollars.

"Happy birthday to me."

CHAPTER 3

By THE TIME I got back to my apartment, I was exhausted.

My head was pounding, my knee ached, and my ribs still hurt when I drew a deep breath. I just wanted to take a long bath with a good book and then sleep until noon.

I parked my car between two abandoned vehicles, tapping their bumpers none-too-gently as I maneuvered into the tight spot. At least half the cars littering the streets of the Outskirts no longer had owners, and many had been broken into and scavenged for parts.

My tiny apartment was in a three-story building that was once identical to its neighbors, though they were now easily distinguished by the graffiti covering their facades. The building I lived in was graced by a thirty-foot-tall painting of a red-nosed clown doing magic. He grinned maniacally down at me as blue flames burst from his fingertips.

Sliding the key in the lock, I grimaced. Thank the gods I

couldn't see that creepy mural from inside the building or I'd never sleep.

I'd lived here for the past eight years, ever since I arrived in Denver. A Gifted man named Edgar had blackmailed me into coming here and working for him to pay off a debt I owed. I'd been under his thumb for five years, until he ended up on the wrong side of the wrong person and got himself killed. Ironically, whoever wanted him dead probably hired someone a lot like me to do the job.

With Edgar out of my life, I could've left Denver... but I wasn't sure where to go. I doubted I'd be welcome anymore in the place I once called home.

The rickety stairs creaked as I made my way up to the top floor. I unlocked the door and was immediately assaulted by the sound of a reality show blaring from the TV.

"Oh my gods, Ivy," I groaned, chucking my keys toward the little table in the corner. I missed, and they slid under the table, but I didn't bother to retrieve them. "Please turn that down."

Ivy turned her heart-shaped face toward me, her shining brown eyes taking in my bedraggled appearance. "Lana! You're home late."

"Ivy. TV. Please," I repeated, stripping off my black jacket and draping it over the back of the couch where she sat.

"Sorry, sorry!" She leaned toward the remote on the coffee table, her finger poised over the volume button. She pressed downward, but her hand passed right through the remote. "Darn. Can you?"

Ivy turned her big doe eyes on me again, and I sighed.

Grabbing the remote, I held the volume button down until my ears were no longer ringing. "There."

"Now it's too quiet," she protested in a small voice, kneeling on the couch so she could peer over the back of it at me. Through her ghostly form, I could see a Gifted woman on the screen being held back by two friends as she threatened to put a hex on a third girl.

I rolled my eyes but bumped the sound up two notches. I had lowered it to nearly silent, because Ivy did this every time. No matter where the volume was set, she always wanted it just a little louder.

"This stuff will rot your brain, you know," I warned her, watching the drama play out on the TV.

"What else am I supposed to do all day?" Ivy turned back around, smoothing her lacy flapper dress down as she did. "I don't know what ghosts did before television was invented. I really don't. I feel sorry for them."

"Trash TV to the rescue."

"Exactly!"

Sinking down onto the couch next to her, I let my eyes slide shut for a minute.

Ivy had come with the apartment, and she hadn't been eager to leave just because a new tenant moved in. For the first year I lived here, she stuck to more traditional haunting, banging cabinets and drawers in the middle of the night, moving my keys around so I could never find them, that kind of thing. But once she realized she wasn't getting rid of me that easily, she came out of hiding and started hanging around more. Eight years in, she was my de facto roommate, although

—thank the gods—she couldn't raid the fridge and eat my food.

I peered over at her. If I looked closely, I could see that she wasn't actually sitting on the couch, but hovering a fraction of an inch over it. She had to focus intensely to make physical contact with corporeal objects, and she could only maintain it for a few seconds.

The ghostly girl noticed my look and tore her gaze away from the TV. "Did you have a bad night? You don't look very good."

Didn't I just have this conversation?

If two people in a row looked at you and immediately asked if you had a rough night, the answer was likely a resounding "yes."

I twisted my hair up into a knot on top of my head, letting cool air hit the back of my neck. "It wasn't the best. A job went sideways, and I won't even break even on it."

"That's too bad. I know you're saving up." Though she continued to talk to me, Ivy's eyes were fixed on the screen again. In a few minutes, I'd lose her entirely.

"Yeah. But I've got another job tomorrow that should make up for it. Hopefully."

"Mm-hm," she murmured absently. "You wanna watch the *Witches versus Warlocks* marathon with me? I'm a few episodes in, but I can catch you up."

"No thanks. I just want to take a hot bath, read for a while, and pass the fuck out."

I hauled my reluctant body up from the couch. Ivy tucked a strand of her short blonde bob behind her ear as she giggled at something on the screen. She probably didn't even realize I'd left. Living with a ghost was a lot like living with a cat. They were pretty low maintenance, but sometimes the relationship felt a little one-sided.

Stifling a yawn, I crossed to the wall opposite the television and perused the large bookshelf.

My apartment was small and dingy, worn down by years of abuse and sporadic repairs. The paint was peeling, the couch was lumpy and full of springs—it was probably a good thing Ivy couldn't actually sit on it—and the table near the kitchen had a two-by-four as one of the legs. The only nice things in the place were the dark oak bookshelf and the treasure trove of books carefully arranged on it. My little library was my pride and joy. I'd read every book at least twice, some more than a dozen times.

Margie, the woman who'd been like a mother to me before Edgar snatched me away from my home in Wyoming, had a penchant for quoting old literature. Thanks to her, I knew most of the famous passages by heart. When I came to Denver, I missed her so much I tracked down copies of her favorite books so I could feel closer to her. Reading became my solace in this strange new city, and I still picked up a book before bed almost every night.

Brushing my fingers over the spines of the volumes lined up neatly on the shelf, I skimmed the titles. I had eighteen of Shakespeare's plays and hoped to complete my collection one day. Books weren't easy to come by for the Blighted though. Most people in the Outskirts were too busy trying to survive to have much interest in reading, and although there were beautiful bookstores inside the Capital, the Gifted proprietors were suspicious of any Blighted person attempting to buy one.

They wanted to keep us dumb and scared. And for the most part, it was working.

I pulled my copy of *Julius Caesar* out and headed to the bathroom.

While the tub filled up with water as hot as I could get it, I stripped off my clothes. I winced when the fabric of my pants slid over my knee, revealing a blooming purple and blue bruise right under the kneecap. A few more bruises decorated my ribs, and my hand was sore from punching both Gerald and his date.

Wiping off the steam gathering on the mirror, I stared at my reflection.

Fuck. I did look rough. My face looked paler than usual, my normally fair skin almost ghostly. Dark circles were visible under my eyes, which had a slightly glazed look. My head still pounded.

Was I getting sick? Or was it just the adrenaline fading from the night I'd had? I didn't normally feel this wiped out after a job. Although, to be fair, most of my jobs went a lot smoother than this one.

Running a finger over the simple quartz necklace I never took off, I stepped into the bath. It was several degrees cooler than I would've liked, but I considered myself lucky to have hot water at all. Sinking into the tub, I let out a low moan of contentment.

I read for a few minutes, careful to keep the book well

away from the bathwater. But I was having a hard time keeping my eyes focused, and the pages kept dipping dangerously close to the water's surface as my head lolled. Finally, I gave up and set the little volume safely on the edge of the sink. I didn't want to accidentally soak one of my favorite books.

Letting my hands float gently on the surface of the water, I spun the copper and tungsten ring around my right middle finger. I slipped it off and peered at the inscription on the inside of the band, reading the numbers I knew by heart.

This was how I knew my twenty-fifth birthday was tomorrow. Or at least why I thought it was.

Twenty years ago, two-thirds of the magical population had suddenly died, wiped out by a plague of unknown origin. The magic users who survived blamed nonmagical people for the plague, assuming that, because they hadn't been struck by the Great Death, they were somehow responsible for it. I'd grown up in a Blighted settlement in the Great Plains of Wyoming, one of dozens of orphaned human children left to fend for ourselves after our families were killed by Gifted lynch mobs.

I didn't know how I'd gotten to Wyoming or who had brought me to the settlement. Though I'd made a family for myself in the Great Plains settlement, I never knew my real parents.

But I thought this ring must have belonged to one of them.

And the numbers inscribed on the inside must be my birthdate.

"Or... maybe I just found it on the ground somewhere

when I was a kid and have been carrying it around all my life for no reason," I muttered, shoving the ring back on my finger and cursing my stupid, sentimental heart.

It was entirely possible I'd scavenged the ring, and the numbers inside were meaningless. I could be turning thirty instead of twenty-five. Hell, my body felt about a hundred right now.

I sighed, sliding down in the tub until my chin hit the top of the water.

What did it really matter if tomorrow was or wasn't my birthday? It wasn't like I was going to throw a party or anything. Still, I liked having a birthdate to mark on the calendar every year.

Even a made up one.

My lids drooped, the headache pounding a steady rhythm in my temples.

GRAY EYES.

Eyes just like mine. Older though, and wet with tears.

A man's large hands engulfed my much smaller ones. His hands shook, which made me afraid. This man shouldn't be scared of anything, but he was frightened now.

His eyes stared straight into me, the gray of his irises seeming to shift and swirl like storm clouds.

Then, like storm clouds heavy with thunder, they lit from within, radiating a piercing white light.

It washed over me, blocking everything else out, almost burning in its intensity.

. . .

WATER WENT UP MY NOSE.

I sputtered, sending a small wave over the edge of the tub as my whole body jerked upright. My heart thudded almost painfully in my chest, and I gripped the edges of the tub as I hacked and coughed, clearing my lungs. I wasn't sure how long I'd dozed, but the water was cold.

Snippets of the dream floated through my still fuzzy mind as I stood up, the cold air on my body making my already chilled skin break out in a riot of goose bumps. I yanked my towel off the rack and wrapped it around myself, stepping out of the water on shaky legs.

"That's it," I muttered, sitting on the tub's edge and pressing my hands to my temples. "No more baths after midnight."

CHAPTER 4

My head still hurt when I woke early the next morning, but it had settled into a dull ache that was entirely ignorable. Which was exactly what I planned to do. I had a job to take care of, and I was determined to make this one go smoothly to redeem myself from the clusterfuck of last night.

I threw on a pair of dark jeans and a long-sleeved black top, then wandered into the kitchen to grab a piece of cold pizza from the ancient, buzzing fridge. How I had survived the first eighteen years of my life without pizza was a mystery. Since I'd come to Denver, it had become a staple of my diet.

Ivy was right where I'd left her, watching a show that toured the houses of the Gifted rich and famous, showing off all their extravagant luxuries.

"Morning, Ivy," I called, holding the pizza slice between my teeth as I crouched under the table to fish out my keys.

Shoving the last few bites in my mouth, I sat on the wobbly folding chair to slip on my boots.

"Good morning." She glanced over at me, her brown eyes wide. "I heard you in the bath last night. You were screaming. Or crying. I couldn't be sure. I thought maybe you were dying."

I looked up, pulling my hair back into a rough ponytail. "Really? Why didn't you come check on me?"

She shrugged. "I couldn't have done much to help. Besides, if you died, you could keep me company forever."

My eyes widened. "Um, Ivy? I don't have to worry about you trying to kill me in my sleep, do I?"

"No, silly! I do think we'd be good friends if you were a ghost though. We could spend whole days together. You're always rushing off to do something or see someone or... I don't know. Whatever the living do."

"But you know not all people who die turn into ghosts, right?" I asked, still a little wary.

Ivy sighed. "I know. A girl can dream though."

"Okay. Just so long as we're clear."

I might have to start locking my bedroom door at night, though it wouldn't really do much to keep her out. I rolled my eyes. *Just another thing ghosts and cats have in common. You never know if they're secretly plotting to kill you.*

"Well, speaking of rushing off to see someone, I gotta go. When I come back tonight five thousand dollars richer, we can watch whatever show you want and celebrate. How about that?"

She nodded exuberantly, her blonde bob flapping. "Yes, please!"

I grabbed my jacket from the back of the couch and slipped it on as I left. The TV volume spiked as soon as the door shut behind me. Funny how she could always manage to use the remote when I wasn't around to do it for her.

The drive to Akio Sun's house took nearly thirty minutes. I rolled past it without slowing down, then pulled to the curb a block away. He lived in Cottage Hill, an area that was nice but nowhere near as extravagant as a lot of the Gifted neighborhoods.

Adjusting my rearview mirror, I kept my eye on the house behind me. It wasn't huge but looked well kept. That made sense. Incubi were known for being incredibly appearance conscious, so even if this Akio guy couldn't afford a giant mansion like the Gifted had, he'd want his place to look nice. It was built in a modern style, with sleek lines and large windows.

And best of all, it didn't appear to be warded.

Gerald's home had been locked down tight with magical wards, but not everyone could afford to do that. If all that stood in my way was a simple deadbolt, this job would be easier than I'd hoped.

I spun the ring on my middle finger idly as I scoped out the house. It didn't look like anyone was home, but I'd still have to play it safe. Slipping on my gloves, I popped the trunk, then hopped out of the car. A mop and a bucket stuffed with rags lay among the various other pieces of equipment in the trunk. I grabbed both and walked straight toward Akio's front door. If any neighbors were watching, hopefully they wouldn't give a second thought to the Blighted housekeeper coming to do some cleaning.

My body tense and alert, I rapped on the door.

No answer.

I waited a minute and knocked again, just to be sure. Still no answer.

The longer I stood on the doorstep, the more suspicious I looked, so I pulled my lock picks from my sleeve and got to work. The deadbolt and the lock on the knob were both ridiculously easy to pick. I'd practiced long enough to be able to pick most standard locks in about the same time it took someone to use a key. As long as I did it confidently enough, I could pick a lock in broad daylight with no witnesses the wiser.

Grabbing my bucket and mop, I slipped inside, my spirits buoyed. This was already going ten times better than last night. Taking down a mark in public was always iffy—my preferred mode of operation was to wait for them somewhere private or follow them home. It wasn't always possible if their house was protected by heavy wards, although there were ways around those if I had the time and money to prepare for them.

I locked the door behind me and drew the rags out of the bucket, revealing my stash of weapons beneath—two small daggers, a nightstick, and a garrote. Rat had said to make Akio's death look accidental if possible, but all my methods of attack were a lot less subtle than that. I'd have to go with option number two and make it look like a botched robbery.

It took less than a minute to arm myself, and then I stuffed the rags back into the bucket and surveyed the house. It was bright, clean, and orderly. The decor was minimal but stylish, with not a single item out of place. This wasn't even close to the smoke-filled sex dungeon I had imagined an incubus would live in.

Or maybe the sex dungeon was in the basement?

I decided not to find out, and instead crept upstairs to the second level. This floor housed a master bedroom, two smaller bedrooms, and a bathroom. I poked my head into each, assessing what would best sell the robbery angle. The whole place was so neat and tidy I cringed at the thought of messing it up.

It probably didn't say anything great about my moral code that I was more ambivalent about destroying a man's possessions than I was about killing him.

"I need to get out of this fucking city," I muttered. Even if I couldn't go back to Wyoming, I needed to make a fresh start somewhere else—soon. I wasn't sure I liked the person I'd become in Denver.

Grimacing, I began methodically creating chaos out of the perfect order of Akio's house. I ripped clothes out of the closet and threw them on the floor. They were all expensive-looking, with a pleasant spicy smell. Next, the comforter came off the bed, tossed haphazardly on the floor. I repeated the actions in the two other bedrooms. They seemed less lived-in than the master bedroom, so there was less to work with, but I did what I could.

I left the first floor as I'd found it, stashing my bucket and mop in the upstairs bathroom. I didn't want Akio to notice any warning signs that something was amiss when he got home. The element of surprise was the best weapon I had.

Patting the daggers at my thighs, I settled in to wait for my date with an incubus.

~

IT WAS NEARLY dusk when Akio returned.

Fucking finally.

I was leaning against the wall just inside the front door when my ears perked at the sound of a car idling outside. A door slammed, and muffled voices floated in from the street.

My headache, which had been mild this morning, was gripping my skull like a vise again. I pressed hard on my temples, trying to quell the throbbing pain. I was definitely getting sick. But there was no time for that now. Once I had five thousand dollars cash in my hand, I could go home and sleep for three days. First, I had to earn it.

The car roared away, and I tensed. A moment later, the lock turned with a *snick* and the door swung open. Akio walked inside, kicking the door shut behind him. Before he could even turn to see me, I leapt on his back, wrapping my legs around his waist and my arms around his neck.

"Wha—!"

The incubus's shout of surprise was cut off as I gripped the bicep of my opposite arm with one hand, squeezing tight across his throat and cutting off his air supply. He let out a low sound, twisting his body to try to shake me off, but I latched on tight, feet hooked together in front of him and arms locked like a vise around his neck.

Now all I had to do was keep my grip on him until he went down.

Akio, of course, had other ideas. Backing up, he slammed me into the wall so hard the plaster cracked. I grunted in pain, my bruised ribs screaming in protest. But I gritted my teeth and tightened my grip on his neck, refusing to let the pain win. His strong hands wrapped around my forearm, trying to pry it free, and for a moment it struck me that he had the same pleasant spicy smell as the clothes in his closet. The scent surrounded me as I clung to him like a burr.

But any thoughts about how good he smelled were driven from my mind as he slammed me against the wall again. Bits of plaster and dust filtered down over me.

Come on, come on...

He couldn't last much longer. But he didn't seem any more inclined to give up than I was. Charging toward the open kitchen, he bashed me against the fridge, the cabinets, the counters. The edge of the counter jabbed into my side and I bit back a scream as pain exploded through my ribs. Broken now, definitely.

Keeping one arm tight around his neck, I scrabbled for my thigh holster with the other and pulled out a dagger, plunging it into his side. His body jerked, and he went to his knees with me still wrapped tightly around him. Leaving the blade in his abdomen, I tightened my chokehold. Grabbing for the dagger had temporarily loosened my grip on his neck, allowing him to pull in small gulps of air. But it had been worth it. I could feel his strength flagging, his body weakening.

There was only one problem.

Mine was too.

Baring my teeth, I tried to push through my exhaustion and the blistering pain in my skull, pouring all my effort into tightening my hold.

But I felt like I was dissolving, melting like a piece of ice on a hot sidewalk. I was having trouble maintaining my grip at all, let alone squeezing tight enough to choke him. My entire body felt hot and numb at the same time, and a sudden wave of nausea swept over me.

Dammit, no! I'm so close. Just go down, you fucker!

Akio was breathing heavily.

Which meant my chokehold was no longer doing anything. Shit.

From somewhere outside myself, I was vaguely aware of sliding down his body, my legs and arms unable to hold me up or support their own weight. The whole room seemed to darken, and Akio had a strange sort of halo around him as he scrambled to his feet, looking down at me, one large hand clasped around the blade still lodged in his side.

"*Akio!*"

It was a new voice. Male. Panicked.

A broad-shouldered figure joined the incubus over my limp body. Or was it two figures? Or three? My vision was hazy, spots dancing across my eyes.

"Shit, Akio, what did you do to her?" one of the men asked, his voice shocked.

"What did I do to *her?*" the incubus gasped. "What about what she did to me? She tried to kill me."

"*What?* Fuck!"

There was a tiny part of my brain that knew how bad this was. A Blighted woman had broken into the home of a Touched man and tried to kill him. If he and his friend— friends?—didn't kill me right now in retribution, I'd be tried and sentenced to death anyway. That part of my mind screamed at me to get up and fight, to run. To do something. *Anything.*

But the little voice in my head was getting smaller and smaller. I couldn't form a complete thought through the pain and disorientation in my mind.

"Sent by the Representatives, you think?" one of the voices asked grimly.

"Possibly. We need to question her. You two, grab her. I'll heal Akio."

The figures standing over me began to move, and I slurred something. I wasn't sure if it was meant to be a plea or a threat, but it hardly mattered; nothing came out but an incoherent moan.

My body blazed with heat, as if I was lying on coals.

Blackness narrowed my vision to a pinprick.

Then everything exploded into white light.

CHAPTER 5

"I say we kill her."

Words filtered into the vast black space I was floating in, echoing like they came through a tunnel from a great distance. I didn't want to leave this dark place yet. It was peaceful and calm here, not terrifying and loud and ugly like the real world so often was.

So I didn't. I just drifted.

"We need to find out who sent her before we do anything else," someone responded. "If it was just an angry husband, that's one thing. If it was the Representatives, that's an entirely different problem."

"Fine. Then can we kill her?"

"Give it up, Akio," a third man said. "You're just salty because she totally got the drop on you."

"Yes." The incubus's voice was smooth and hard. "Being attacked in my home, choked, and stabbed does have the effect of making me a bit *salty*."

"Well, she hit us all with something too," the third man argued. "What the hell was that, Jae?"

"I don't know. I can't get a read on her power."

The men continued to speak, and every word that penetrated the darkness of my mind dragged me further away from the safe, quiet place. Instead of floating weightlessly, I was plunged back into the heaviness of my body. I lay on something firm and padded, and my arms were above my head, tingling in a vaguely uncomfortable way. My mind felt fuzzy and sluggish, making it hard to piece together what happened. How had I gotten here?

I dragged my eyelids up, flicking my gaze around the room. I was in a bedroom, I realized. On a large bed.

As the fog lifted, I shifted slightly to reassure myself all my limbs were still attached.

"Hey!" one of the men called, catching the attention of the other two.

They stopped bickering immediately, and silence fell over the room.

I swallowed.

Three sets of eyes stared intently at me.

Akio, the incubus I'd been sent to kill, glared at me with eyes so dark they were nearly black. I'd expected him to be handsome—he was an incubus, after all. But his beauty was so striking it almost hurt to look at. His skin was a deep tan that looked smooth as silk, which only highlighted his sharp, chiseled features. It was the most stunningly perfect face I'd ever seen, and I wondered briefly if he looked like this before he became an incubus, or if his demon nature had enhanced his appeal somehow. Even with his eyes shooting daggers at me, I didn't want to look away.

When I finally did, my jaw almost dropped.

Was I surrounded by incubi?

Akio's two friends were as different from him and each other as could be, but they were both unreasonably handsome too.

The one sitting on the bed next to me had a long, straight nose, light brown hair, and piercing green eyes that seemed to see right through me. He regarded me with careful curiosity, and I thought I could see a bit of empathy hidden in his expression. I made note of that. If I was going to get out of this alive, I needed to get at least one of these guys on my side. He might be that one. Besides, there was something about him that put me at ease, something I innately wanted to trust—and I didn't trust anybody.

Hovering over his shoulder, head bobbing side to side like an overexcited puppy, was a man with messy dark hair, thick eyebrows, and a bit of scruff framing his full lips.

As soon as my gaze fell on him, his chocolate brown eyes lit up, and he grinned widely. "Good morning, killer!"

Akio, who leaned against the wall by the door, snorted. "Please don't sound so happy about my attempted assassination, Fenris. I might take it the wrong way."

The scruffy man shrugged. "You take everything the wrong way."

I sat up quickly—or tried to. The restraints binding my wrists to the headboard went tight, yanking me back down to the plush mattress. I twisted to peer up at my bonds, then stopped suddenly.

My ribs had definitely been broken. Now I moved and breathed with ease.

I looked back at the men, all three of whom still watched me intently. "Did you... did you heal me?"

"Jae did." Fenris inclined his head toward the delicate-featured man sitting beside me.

"Yes," Jae admitted. "You had several broken ribs."

I blinked. "Wait, you're not all incubi?"

Fenris tilted his head back and howled with laughter. "*All* incubi? No, thank the gods. Akio is enough. Can you imagine the ego overload if all of us were incubi? There wouldn't be room for anything else in the house!"

Akio scowled, tilting his head at a perfect angle, like a model posing. I wasn't even sure he knew he was doing it.

"So what are you?" As soon as the words were out of my mouth, I realized I didn't need to ask. I knew. I could *feel* the power coming off them. Jae was a mage—and a strong one. Fenris was a...

"Shifter." Fenris grinned, confirming my suspicion.

"Mage," Jae added solemnly.

"Incubus." Akio shot the word at me like a poison dart.

Shit. I was in a room with three powerful Gifted and Touched men. Wait, scratch that. I was *tied up* in a room with three magical men, at least one of whom had good reason to hate me.

How the hell was I still alive?

"Don't take this the wrong way," I said slowly, my voice

gaining strength as I shook off the last vestiges of fog in my mind. "But... why did you heal me?"

"I've been wondering the exact same thing, actually," Akio said coldly.

Ignoring him, I focused on Jae, choosing my words carefully. "I'm not ungrateful for your mercy. But I know how the world works. Every bit of kindness comes at a cost. So, what's the price?"

Remembering my earlier imaginings of a sex dungeon in the basement, I suppressed a shiver. All three of them were attractive men, but I had no interest in selling my body for my freedom.

Jae cocked his head at me, regarding me with intense eyes. "I healed you because you were hurt. There is no price."

"Yeah?" His reassurance didn't do much to quell the panic rising in my chest. "Then why am I tied up? What do you want from me?"

Please, gods. I spent years under Edgar's thumb. Don't let it happen again.

"Relax. Please." Jae held a hand up soothingly. "I promise no harm will come to you. But tell me, who sent you? Why did you attack Akio?"

If I had a name to give him, I would've blurted it out without a second thought. Let the damned Gifted all kill each other with their petty squabbles and power plays.

My nose scrunched up before I admitted, "I don't know. I have a contact person, a guy called Rat. I don't even know his real name. He brings jobs from his Gifted clients to me and a few other mercenaries in the city. Collection jobs, sometimes thefts or setups. Not usually assassinations." I shot a guilty look at Akio, expecting another caustic remark, but the incubus remained silent.

"You're a mercenary?" Jae shifted on the bed, sharing a look with Fenris. "You don't work with the Representatives?"

I scoffed. "The government? No, I don't work with them."

When the Great Death struck, it had wiped out most of the Presidential line of succession. After a short period of chaos and disorder, a few Gifted leaders stepped in to fill the power vacuum. What emerged over the next decade was the Order of Magic, a single-party system governed by a council of seven Representatives and presided over by the Secretary General, a man named Theron Stearns. Who they were supposed to be "representing," I had no idea. Only the Gifted and Touched were allowed to vote. And there hadn't been an election in years.

"A Gifted mercenary," Jae muttered, almost to himself. "I can't believe I haven't heard of you before. You're powerful enough to draw attention. I should've known about you."

"I'm not..." I shook my head, confused. "I'm not Gifted."

Akio rolled his eyes, pressing away from the wall to stalk toward me. "I told you you wouldn't get anything but lies from her, Jae."

"I'm not lying, you asshole! I'm one of the Blighted. Sorry if your poor little ego can't handle a Blighted girl getting the drop on you"—I purposely echoed Fenris's words, and was rewarded by the slight flush that crept up Akio's tan cheeks —"but that's exactly what happened."

Akio stopped next to the bed, staring down at me. I

couldn't stop my gaze from sliding down his body, checking for evidence of my attack. His throat was smooth and corded with muscle, but I didn't see any bruises; he'd changed out of his blazer and white tee into a dark blue long-sleeved shirt, which was clear of blood. Jae must have healed him too.

"That's not *exactly* what happened." Akio's voice was a mixture of velvet and steel.

I shook my head, not understanding what he meant. If he wanted to keep insisting I hadn't gotten the better of him, I supposed I should let him. Maybe a little ego stroking would help get me out of this.

And, a little voice in the back of my head reminded me, *you did lose the fight.*

But I'd only lost because I'd been sick. Jae must have healed my fever when he took care of my ribs, thank the gods.

"You released a blast of magic," the mage said softly, pulling my attention back to him. His green eyes were clear and bright as he studied me. "I've never felt anything like it. You knocked all of us out for several minutes. When we came to, you were out cold. You stayed that way for almost twenty-four hours."

My breath hitched. "What? No, that's not…."

I trailed off, wracking my brain for an explanation. Had one of my magical gadgets gone haywire? That didn't make any sense. I didn't have many charmed toys left. I'd used my transport spell last night, and my cuffs were gone. And I'd never heard of magic accidentally exploding from a charmed object.

Was he lying to me? Had he been the one to release the magic, and now he was trying to pin it on me?

"I'm Blighted." My voice wavered. "I'm not Gifted. I've never done magic in my life. Whatever happened, it wasn't me."

"Oh, it was definitely you, killer. We were all there; we felt it happen. Hell, I can still feel it." Fenris rubbed his chest, looking pensive for the first time since I'd met him.

I shook my head adamantly. "I'm not. I'm not one of the fucking Gifted. I'm not part of your psycho little magic club, okay? I don't get off on oppressing people or think I'm better than anyone with less power than me."

As the possibility sank in, my voice rose in volume and pitch. This wasn't possible. I couldn't be one of the Gifted. I'd spent my life hating them, and I refused to accept that I could be one of their ranks.

But even as I spoke, I couldn't shake the feeling that something felt different. Unfamiliar power burned low and steady in the pit of my stomach, like someone had turned on a pilot light inside me.

Fenris elbowed Jae. "Huh, where have I heard that before?"

Jae nodded, eyeing me intently. "You don't like the Gifted very much, do you?"

"Why should I?" I countered bitterly. I was probably digging my own grave by insulting him and his kind, but I hardly cared about that anymore. A quick death didn't sound so bad at the moment. Whatever strange ride I was on, I wanted to get off. "The Gifted killed my family, took me away from the only man I ever loved, and treat me like a disposable tool. They bicker and play power games, and the ones who pay the worst price for it are the Blighted."

I cut off my tirade before I built up an unstoppable head of steam.

If I'd thought my words would offend them, I couldn't have been more wrong. Fenris was beaming at me, and even Akio's expression had softened a bit.

"This is incredible!" Fenris bounced on his toes. "She could be exactly what we've been looking for, Jae! It doesn't even matter what she can do. Packing that kind of power, she can—"

He cut off when a fourth man entered the room, tucking a cell phone into his back pocket as he rounded the doorframe.

"I checked in with Christine. They haven't picked up any chatter about the Representatives putting a price on Akio's head. It was probably a private job, but she...."

The new man trailed off, his gaze catching mine. Clear blue eyes stopped my breath. His face was leaner and more grown-up than when I'd last seen him, his features harder. His sandy blond hair was shorter, cropped tight to his head.

But his eyes were exactly the same.

I finally found my voice.

"Corin?"

CHAPTER 6

THE OTHER THREE men glanced between me and Corin in apparent confusion. But I barely registered their surprised looks. My heart banged against my ribs as if it wanted to escape my chest. My face felt hot, and tears burned the backs of my eyes.

A dozen different emotions crashed around inside me, creating a jumble of thoughts and feelings I couldn't begin to sort through.

Joy. Confusion. Hope.

But one emotion rose above all the others, almost choking me with its strength.

Guilt.

I was sure my face was flushed, my eyes glassy.

"Corin?" I whispered again, the word hardly more than a breath.

"Hi, Lana."

The man I'd once known better than anyone gave me a

curt nod, as if greeting an old acquaintance he hadn't liked very much. His expression was shuttered, his eyes carefully impassive.

My shock over being told I was Gifted paled in comparison to what I was feeling now. After crying myself to sleep every night for months when I'd first come to Denver, I'd forced myself to tuck my memories of Corin into a little vault in my heart, keeping them safe but out of reach.

His arrival had just taken a stick of dynamite and blown up the entire vault. Memories rushed out in a torrent, making my head spin and my heart ache.

"Wait!" Fenris narrowed his eyes at Corin, bounding across the room toward him. "You *know* her?" When Corin didn't respond, his gaze still glued to my face, Fenris pressed, "You didn't think to mention that?"

"I don't know her," Corin said stiffly. "I *knew* her. A long time ago."

"Still an important piece of information to share with your teammates, don't you think?"

The dark-haired shifter looked back at me, an expression almost like envy flitting over his features. Was he jealous that his friend had a previous connection to me?

Corin's words cut deep, the sting only made more painful by the fact that I knew I deserved them. And far worse.

An expectant silence hung in the air, but Corin seemed in no hurry to break it. The shifter looked back and forth between us, dark brown eyes wide.

"What... what are you doing here?" I finally asked, unable to stop myself. "When did you come to Denver? Is Margie—?"

"She's dead." He swallowed, blinking rapidly. "Died a couple years after you left."

My heart dropped. She'd been like a mother to him since he was six, and had taken me under her wing too. I thought of her sweet face, her wrinkled, paper-thin skin, and short white hair glowing like a halo around her head. Margie had been one of the best people I'd ever known—kind and gentle, but fierce as hell.

"I'm so sorry, Corin."

He shook his head slightly. "She died peacefully. I was there to watch over her and keep her safe."

I winced. That dig hurt too. I *hadn't* been there for her, but it seemed pointless to explain to him that I had wanted to be, with all my heart.

"I'm sorry," Akio interjected. "But would you mind explaining exactly how it is you know the woman someone hired to kill me?"

Corin cleared his throat, finally wrenching his gaze away from me. "It's a long story."

Akio crossed his arms and arched one eyebrow. "I've got nothing but time."

"Unfortunately, we don't. Christine wants us to bring her in for questioning."

Shit. That didn't sound good. The last time I'd been "brought in for questioning" by one of the Gifted, I'd ended up in indentured servitude to him for years. Was that why Corin was here? Had these men blackmailed or coerced him into serving them? They weren't talking to him like an underling. In fact, if I hadn't known him for years and been certain he was Blighted, I would have thought he was one of them. They treated him like an equal.

"Can we trust her?" Jae, who had been silently observing our exchange, stood and turned to Corin.

The blond man scrubbed a hand over the back of his neck in a familiar gesture. He'd been unable to tear his eyes away from me when he first entered the room, but now it seemed he couldn't bring himself to look at me. Finally, he sighed, shaking his head. "I don't know."

A tiny flicker of anger rose above the guilt I felt. It was true Corin had plenty of reasons not to trust me, but he had to know telling a roomful of Gifted and Touched men that he wasn't sure I was trustworthy put me in mortal danger. I'd seen Blighted people sentenced to death based on an accusation alone. If these men thought I was a threat, they could put me down without a second thought and face no consequences for it.

"I'm not going to try to kill any of you," I blurted. "You've got me outnumbered, and I'm not stupid. And my contract for the incubus is null now anyway."

Akio snorted.

Jae regarded me thoughtfully for a moment. Then he bent over the bed, fiddling with the restraints that bound my wrists. With a soft click, they popped open.

I was so stunned I just lay there, staring up at him. He glanced down and caught my eyes. His face wasn't a mask like Corin's was, but I still couldn't read it. He was clearly very intelligent; it was as if his expression was a thought too complex for me to understand.

My breath caught in my throat, and only when Jae stood did my lungs find the space to pull in a long drag of air.

I sat up slowly, rubbing my wrists and working out the kinks in my tingling arms.

"What are you doing?" Akio had been leaning against the side of the headboard, but he straightened indignantly. "Have we all lost sight of the fact that she tried to kill me?"

"Of course not," Jae said, stepping back to let me have some space.

Akio didn't seem inclined to do me the same courtesy. He towered over me, his disapproving glare practically burning a hole in my skull. "Then why—?"

"She said it herself. We have her outnumbered, and she has no reason to kill you anymore. She's a hired gun, not the operator behind the curtain. And if we want her to help us, we need to stop treating her like a prisoner. Having another powerful Gifted person on our side could change everything."

"I'm not Gifted," I repeated, though it felt like giving up the one trump card I carried. A sudden thought occurred to me, and I gestured to Corin. "Ask him, he knows! I'm Blighted. We grew up in the same human settlement together."

Everyone looked back at Corin. He flushed, obviously uncomfortable being put on the spot again.

"I thought you were, Lana. I really did. But..." His voice trailed off, his brows drawing together. "But what you unleashed yesterday was magic of some kind. I'm sure of that."

"That can't be!"

"I was there, Lana. It happened." He dipped his head, looking almost sorry for me.

The irony of him pitying me for the discovery I might be Gifted wasn't lost on me. If it were true, it would automatically elevate me in society. I could get a real job—one that didn't involve stealing, fighting, or cooking and cleaning for the citizens of the Capital. I could go where I wanted, when I wanted, without fear of getting randomly stopped and questioned by Peacekeepers.

But it would also mean everything I thought I knew about myself was wrong. That who I was, down to the very core of my being, was a mystery to me. The only person in the room who could understand the pain and confusion of this revelation was Corin. The Blighted had it bad; there was no denying that. But that didn't mean I hadn't been proud of what I was.

Now? I had no idea what I was.

As it usually did when I was this confused and overwhelmed, my fight-or-flight impulse kicked into high gear. I'd told Jae I wouldn't try to kill anyone, but the instinct to lash out, to get out of here or die trying, was strong.

I jerked to my feet on shaky legs, my eyes darting around the room.

As soon as I stood, all four men tensed, their eyes tracking my every movement. They could probably read the panic on my face.

"Lana," Jae said softly. "Breathe."

My wild gaze landed on him, and it was only when he said it that I realized my lungs were burning, desperate for air.

"It… can't be," I gasped. "I'm not—"

My skin was growing hot again. *Oh, fuck. No.*

"Breathe."

Jae's voice was like a balm, washing over me and cooling my burning skin. The other three stayed alert and on edge, but seemed to defer to him in this.

I sucked in another ragged breath, fighting the darkness that edged my vision. I suddenly felt the urge to weep, to cry until I had no more tears left, as if I had too much of *something* inside me and it needed a release.

Moving slowly and deliberately, Jae reached toward me.

I stood frozen like a rabbit on an empty plain, searching for a threat, certain one was out there.

His hand grasped mine.

The connection made me jump, but as soon as his cool, long fingers touched my skin, the roiling heat building up inside me like lava began to dissipate. I tightened my grip, clinging to his hand like a lifeline.

"There," he breathed. "You're all right. Your magic is agitated. It's responding very strongly to your emotions right now. Try to stay calm."

That was an impossible directive to follow, but I nodded anyway.

Everyone exhaled a collective breath, the tension in the room lessening.

"You really didn't know you were Gifted, did you?" Jae's voice was soft, his fine lips pursed as he studied me.

I shook my head.

"That explains the magic you let out," Fenris interjected helpfully. "You probably didn't even mean to do it, killer."

"I'm sure she didn't. She's untrained. Completely."

"Excuse me for saying so," Akio said. "But I don't see how having an untrained mage on our side is the coup you think it is, Jae. How helpful can she be if she can't even use her powers?"

I chose to ignore the incubus, and everyone else seemed content to go along with that decision. I looked to the other three. "You keep saying 'on our side.' What does that mean, exactly? Side of what?"

"We're part of the Resistance." Fenris grinned at me.

"The... what?"

"The Resistance. An underground group trying to bring down the Gifted establishment. We're fighting for equality among the races."

My jaw dropped. "What?"

"Oh, are we telling her everything now? Nice, Fenris. Why don't you just show her the secret handshake while you're at it?" Akio threw his hands up and flopped onto the bed. Even in his irritation, the movement was graceful as a cat.

"I'm not telling her anything she wouldn't find out soon anyway. Corin already said Christine wants us to bring her in."

"Speaking of which," Corin added, still avoiding my eyes. "We better get going."

Jae squeezed me hand, making me realize we were still connected. When he loosened his grip, I pulled my hand back quickly. That had felt way too comfortable.

"We won't force you to help us, but if you're willing, we could use someone like you," he said. "Very few of the Gifted or Touched have much interest in joining a rebellion against the same government that grants them such unilateral power. There are only a few others like us in the Resistance, and although I don't have any doubts about the strength and capabilities of our nonmagical members, sometimes it helps to fight fire with fire—or magic with magic."

"And if I say no?"

I wasn't sure I wanted to say no. What Fenris had described sounded incredible. But I'd been on my own for so long that the idea of joining a group, even for a cause I believed in, made me feel itchy and anxious. Attachments were a weakness. I'd learned that years ago, just like Corin had.

"We'll make the case for leniency for your attack on Akio if you pledge your dedication to the Resistance and agree to help us. I can't say for certain what Christine will decide to do, but I can promise I won't let her hurt you. Even if you choose not to join us," Jae said, his green eyes shining with sincerity.

"Neither will I." Fenris almost growled the words, the protectiveness in his voice startling me. I could almost picture hackles rising on his back and wondered dazedly if he was a wolf shifter.

Against every rational, cynical instinct I had, I believed them.

I didn't really have a choice. But I appreciated them making me feel like I did.

"Okay." I nodded. "Let's go see Christine."

CHAPTER 7

As it turned out, the car that had roared down the street to drop Akio off the day before belonged to Jae.

Of course it did. It was hardly surprising that the sleek, expensive-looking silver vehicle belonged to the mage.

Leave it to the Gifted to—

I cut myself off midthought. I needed to stop thinking this way. That group included me now, something my brain could hardly process. It also included Jae, and despite his obnoxiously fancy car, he actually seemed like a good, honorable man. I had plenty of verifiable evidence that most of the Gifted were self-interested, power-hungry bigots, but maybe I'd been wrong to paint the whole group with one brush.

Akio had ushered us out through the main floor of his house. Dried blood stained the floor and cabinets in the kitchen, the fridge was tilted off its axis, and there was a crater in the plaster by the front door. I carefully avoided looking at any of it, while Akio kept his resentful stare pinned on me.

Jae's car wasn't large, and none of these men were small, so it would've been a challenge for all three of the other guys to fit in the back.

That was how I somehow ended up sandwiched in the middle seat between Akio and Fenris.

I sat stiffly, my body completely still, trying to pull my atoms closer together to avoid touching either one of them. The coldness coming from the incubus was a startling contrast to the warmth radiating from the shifter. Both sensations were confusing and unwelcome. I didn't trust Akio, and he sure as hell didn't trust me. That made me want to lean into Fenris, and *that* made me not trust myself.

Corin and Jae talked in low tones in the front seat as we drove through the Capital. I tried to pick up on what they were saying, but I was so hyperfocused on the two men sitting next to me I could hardly hear over the rush of blood in my ears.

Fenris noticed my tension but misinterpreted the cause, patting my knee before saying, "There's nothing to worry about, killer. Christine is tough, but she's fair. And she's smart. She won't throw away a possible ally just to get revenge."

He reached over my shoulder to poke Akio as he said that last part, and the other man muttered something under his breath, turning to stare out the window.

The scruffy shifter left his arm where it was, resting casually across the seat behind me. I remained stiff as a board, breathing shallowly in case too much rib expansion made me accidentally brush up against him. Fenris's casually familiar treatment of me made me uneasy—mostly because it didn't feel strange.

I'd never been the friendliest person, but my time in Denver had pushed me toward what could best be described as "standoffish." I didn't make friends easily and had no interest in spending time with or conversing with strangers. As far as I was concerned, the only reason people interacted was because they each wanted something from the other person. And I didn't want to owe anything to or need anything from anyone.

But these men confused me. They did want something from me—my help, whatever good that might do—but they didn't seem interested in coercing or manipulating me to get it. Years ago, I'd known Corin better than anyone, but somehow I felt as if I'd known the others that long too. Like I had known them in another life, and an unconscious part of me instantly recognized them as old friends.

I gulped.

This was so not like me.

Clearing my throat, I glanced at Fenris out of the corner of my eye. "Where are we going?"

"Resistance headquarters. It's in the Outskirts." He cocked his head to the side like a dog. *Yep, wolf shifter. Definitely.* "You've really never heard of us?"

I leaned back, relaxing slightly. "I've heard rumors. I didn't know it was an actual organization. I just thought it was individual people getting fed up with life under Gifted rule and acting on their own. Sorry."

Fenris chuckled, a deep, warm sound that poured over me like chocolate. "Don't be sorry, killer. We try to keep out of the headlines. It's a balancing act between recruiting supporters and staying off the government's radar. The more they know about what we're doing, the more often things like your attempted hit on Akio will happen."

Akio heaved a sigh, and I almost laughed. He was one of the most dramatic people I'd ever met.

A twinge of guilt snuck up on me. I *had* tried to kill him. I supposed if the roles had been reversed, and he'd sneak-attacked me in my apartment, I wouldn't be in a hurry to forgive and forget either.

"And why are you all part of it? The Resistance? I wouldn't think most of you would be anxious to change the status quo."

Jae and Corin had stopped talking up front and were listening in on our conversation. I tried not to keep sneaking glances at Corin, but it was hard to resist. He looked so much like the boy I'd known, but the world had changed him—just like it had changed me. I wanted to study his face for hours, until the memory of him and the real flesh and blood Corin in front of me blended back into the same person.

"I can't speak for the others. They'll have to tell you their own stories. But I can tell you why I joined." Fenris's voice pulled me from my thoughts. The fingertips of his arm resting on the back of the seat brushed my shoulders, and though my body tensed again, I didn't move away. "When the Great Death hit, it wiped out a lot of my pack, including my parents.

The ones who didn't die splintered off. No one could agree on who to blame or how to move forward. Eventually, it tore us apart, and the pack dissolved. I moved into the city and have been packless ever since."

He shook his head, his body vibrating with agitation. "I know the Touched don't have it as bad as the Blighted, but we don't have it good either. Packs and prides are being pulled apart everywhere. Shifters are being recruited by rich mages, witches, and warlocks as hired muscle for their own ends. We're just glorified security guards to the fucking Gifted." He paused, then kicked the back of Jae's chair lightly. "No offense."

"None taken," Jae said calmly from the front seat, a note of amusement in his voice.

I could barely conceal my shock at how easily Jae let go of the insult. It was clear the four men in this car were friends, but most of the Gifted I'd met had an extremely low tolerance for any perceived slight. I'd always attributed it to the fact that deep down, they knew they weren't any better than the Blighted or Touched. To maintain the illusion of their superiority, they had to constantly enforce it.

"Anyway, I was working as a bartender at Sparks, a club in the Capital, when Christine recruited me. Been working with the Resistance ever since. I brought Corin on board about three years ago."

My eyes flashed up to the front seat, curiosity burning. Corin had been here for three years? I couldn't believe we'd been in the same city for this long and not known it. After Edgar died, I'd thought about going back to Wyoming so many times, but I'd never been able to work up the courage to face Corin after what I'd done to him. I'd entertained wild dreams of saving enough money for us to start over someplace peaceful, but even though I stashed away a bit of my earnings from every job, it never seemed like enough.

Not enough to make up for breaking his heart.

A slight flush rose in Corin's cheeks as he felt my eyes on him. I watched him expectantly, hoping he'd pipe up next with the story of how he'd joined this mysterious Resistance, but he drew his lips into a thin line, staring straight ahead.

My heart sank.

I'd imagined dozens of ways we might be reunited, but the circumstances I currently found myself in had never entered my mind. I wasn't prepared for this—didn't know the right words to say that would break down the walls he'd put up around himself.

The car lapsed into silence as we rolled out of the Capital.

Fenris's thumb absently rubbed the curve of my shoulder, and although I'd never admit it out loud, the small contact was very comforting. I had the strangest urge to lean into his touch, to let him wrap his arm fully around me and nuzzle into his neck, soaking up the warmth and musk of his skin. The little spark of light deep inside me flared brighter at the thought. My magic—if that was truly what it was—seemed to want to get closer to him.

The derelict buildings of the Outskirts slid past us as Jae drove through an area I didn't know. It appeared to be mostly abandoned, with more crumbling and burned-out buildings than whole ones. We passed by a house that nature was slowly reclaiming; half the roof was missing, and the top of a tree was poking through the hole.

These parts of the Outskirts were filled with squatters. My apartment was shitty, but it had heat and running water, and I paid rent to live there. Here, people sought shelter in whatever buildings weren't totally destroyed, either sharing the space with others or fighting them for dominance.

A woman dressed in rags and clutching a baby to her chest watched us pass, the whites of her wide eyes standing out starkly in her dirty face.

I shifted uncomfortably in my seat.

Jae's car stood out like a sore thumb. My ugly-ass Honda Accord drew the attention of Gifted law enforcement, but it'd fit right in here in the Outskirts. I wasn't used to drawing stares from my fellow Blighted.

No. Not my fellow Blighted. Not anymore.

My gut twisted at the thought of people I'd once considered my kind looking at me with the disgust and fear usually reserved for the Gifted. I could feel my heart rate speeding up, panic and anger rising in my chest again.

Jae's head flicked up, glancing at me in the rearview mirror.

"Fenris," he said quietly.

The shifter squeezed my shoulder. "It's okay, killer. We're almost there. Just take it easy."

Like I'd done with Jae's help earlier, I drew in a few deep breaths. Fenris's touch was comforting, although it didn't provide the same immediate calming relief as Jae's had.

We drove another mile until the buildings began to thin

out, spreading farther and farther away from each other. Jae finally pulled over in front of a derelict duplex. "Here we are."

Akio popped his door and slid out in one smooth motion. Fenris held the other door open for me, offering his hand to help me out.

I stared at it blankly for a moment. I wasn't used to chivalrous gestures, and I'd certainly never had a hard time getting out of a car before. I wasn't sure whether to be touched or insulted that he thought I needed help.

Finally, I took it, allowing him to tug me gently from the car. Now wasn't the time to insult my captors—though I had to keep reminding myself that's what they were. They treated me so well it was hard to remember sometimes. Bitterly, I wondered if I'd be dead already if they weren't convinced I was Gifted. If I were just a Blighted woman who'd broken into Akio's house to attack one of them, would they have taken any mercy on me?

Wind rustled the leaves of the trees and shrubs that filled the space where houses had once stood. Jae made a gesture with his hand, and a faint glow flared up around his car. A ward.

Akio led the way up the crumbling cement steps to the duplex. The doorknob was missing, and the door was slightly ajar. It opened with a high-pitched squeak. I crossed the threshold after Corin, my eyes adjusting to the dimly lit space.

This was the Resistance headquarters?

It can't be. There's nothing here.

The interior of the building was choked with dust. Light filtering in through the dirty windows caught the particles stirred up by our entrance, making them glitter. There was a heaviness in the air, as if the space had been closed up for a long time.

I glanced at the men around me, my hands curling into fists. Why would they bring me *here*? Had they lied to me? Was there no Resistance after all?

CHAPTER 8

I WAS A GODSDAMNED IDIOT. I couldn't believe I'd actually trusted the word of fucking magic users.

But I didn't understand why they'd gone to the trouble of this elaborate lie. If they were going to kill me—or worse—they could've done it back at Akio's place.

Unless he didn't want to ruin his nice sheets.

Fear washed over me like a bucket of ice water, chilling my skin even as sweat dampened my brow.

Akio walked confidently toward the back of the house. Farther away from the windows, the interior plunged into murky darkness. Thick cobwebs covered the broken furniture and crisscrossed over the corners of doorframes. The only person behind me was Jae. I hung back, slowing my pace until he drew up alongside me.

Then I pivoted and bolted toward the front door.

My heavy footfalls sent up clouds of dust as I heard someone shout behind me. Just as I reached the door, a body slammed into me, strong arms wrapping around me in a bear hug.

I kicked back, aiming a stomp at Corin's insole, but he shifted his weight to avoid my strike. His thick, muscled arms tightened around me, and I could feel his breath on my ear.

"Lana, don't run. No one here wants to hurt you, but we can't let you go. Not until you talk to Christine."

My body knew this position, remembered perfectly the feel of his arms around me, and against my will, my muscles relaxed.

"How could you do this, Corin?" I whispered. "I know I hurt you, but why—?"

"I'm not going to let anything happen to you. We're just taking you to see Christine. I promise." His voice was rough in my ear, but this was the first time since he walked into Akio's bedroom that he talked to me like a real person.

"Where is she, then? This place is fucking abandoned."

"The entrance is hidden. We have to be careful. The Representatives have been getting more aggressive lately, trying to find us and stamp us out."

I could feel his heart thudding against my back. Could he feel mine jumping like a jackrabbit?

"Corin, how did—?"

"If you two are quite done," Akio called from the back of the house. "I thought we were in a hurry."

As if realizing what he was doing, Corin dropped his arms quickly and stepped back. "We should get moving."

My body immediately missed his warmth, but I straightened my spine, turning slowly to face the others.

Fenris and Jae watched us from either side of a doorway at the back of the space, their faces illuminated by the soft ball of light that hovered over Jae's outstretched hand. Akio was halfway down the stairs leading to the basement, wearing an impatient expression.

Without looking at me, Corin grabbed my arm and tugged me toward the basement door. I didn't resist.

As we entered the dark basement, a musty, decayed smell assaulted my nose, making me sneeze. Something in the corner caught my eye. A section of the wall shimmered in the glow of Jae's light, wavering like a ripple on the surface of a pond.

A portal.

So this wasn't the Resistance headquarters, just a way to get to them.

As if reading my thoughts, Jae explained. "There are a handful of portals leading to the Resistance spaced throughout the Outskirts. I move the portals every few weeks to keep the Representatives from being able to trace our movements. If Resistance members returned to the same place too often, it would be easier for the government to track them and find our base."

That made sense. And I could see now why they valued having a few of the Gifted on their side. Something like this wouldn't be possible if the Resistance was comprised entirely of Blighted people. As much as I hated magic users, magic itself could be incredibly useful.

"I haven't attuned the portal to you, so you'll have to step through with me. Later, I can key you in so you'll be able to come and go as you please," Jae added.

"Assuming Christine decides she'll be useful," Akio muttered before stepping through the portal. I was tempted to give him a little help by kicking his ass as he passed through. *Dick.*

Fenris stepped through next, followed by Corin, who almost turned his head to glance back at me but arrested the movement.

Jae held out his free hand, palm up, and looked at me. I swallowed. I almost would've preferred he grabbed my arm like Corin had. Taking his offered hand felt strangely intimate.

His long fingers closed around mine, his skin smooth and cool.

Like a king escorting his queen down a promenade, he walked beside me into the portal. We passed through the shimmering section of the dirty basement wall… into another dark and musty space.

Not a big improvement, as far as I was concerned.

"This is it?" I asked, trying to keep the disappointment out of my voice.

Fenris chuckled, his eyes gleaming in the light of Jae's orb. "You ain't seen nothin' yet, killer. Come on."

The space we were in turned out to be an abandoned tunnel. We followed it for several minutes, making a few twists and turns as we passed other faintly glowing portals. I took careful note of our path in case I had to retrace my steps in a hurry. Finally, Jae snuffed his glowing magic orb as the tunnel opened up into a wider room. Two Blighted men sat at a folding table, playing a game of cards by lantern light. At the sight of us, they abandoned the game and scrambled to their feet, standing at attention.

Corin nodded to them. "As you were."

"Yes, sir." The older of the two men, who had a thick beard and a wicked scar over his left eye, stared suspiciously at me. "She one of the Gifted?"

How the hell did he know that? Was I radiating power like all Gifted did? I couldn't feel it coming from myself, but I'd been around enough magic users to know they were impossible to miss.

"Yes," Jae said. "Christine wants to meet her. She may be able to help us."

I noticed he didn't mention the other reason this Christine woman wanted to meet me—the fact that I'd attacked one of their members.

The man tugged his beard as he considered Jae's words for a moment. Then he stepped aside. "Keep a close eye on her, sir. She's awfully powerful; I can tell that from here," he muttered, loud enough for us all to hear.

"Thank you, Abel." Jae's voice was cool.

The other guard pulled the door open for us, and we stepped through into what looked like an abandoned factory. Large metal cylinders loomed around us, and sharp beams of sunlight cut through the gloom from high, partially boarded-up windows.

People crossed through the space, on their way to do who-knew-what, but every one of them stopped to stare at us.

Or more specifically, at me.

Shit. If this was what being Gifted was like, I hated it already. My flame red hair made me stand out in any crowd, but that was easily solved by a cap. I'd made my living by being able to blend in, to become unremarkable and invisible. But somehow I doubted there was a hat that would disguise the magic inside me.

The four men spaced themselves out around me, two in front and two behind, like an honor guard. For once, I didn't mind their closeness. The looks I was getting from the people here weren't openly hostile, but they weren't warm. Suspicion tinged the face of every person who met my gaze.

Fenris grabbed the arm of a young boy passing by. "Hey, Trev, go get Christine, will you? Tell her to meet us in the war room."

The boy's eyes widened, and he shot a glance at me before scampering away.

"Friendly place," I muttered.

"You'll get used to it," Jae said softly. "The stares. Once they know they can trust you, it won't be so bad."

We passed through a giant warehouse that had been transformed into a barracks, with hundreds of cots and blankets laid out in orderly rows, before entering another section of the factory. This one had an office area one level above, overlooking the main floor. Probably the old foreman's office. We tromped up the rusty metal steps single file. The walls of the office had once been floor-to-ceiling glass, but all the panes except one were broken now. Pieces of cloth were tacked across the openings, undulating lightly in the drafts of air slipping into the factory. The dirty glass of the single remaining window revealed a woman inside the office, leaning against a broad wooden table.

Jae rapped one knuckle on the door and opened it without waiting for a response.

The office had been mostly gutted, leaving a large open space. The only piece of furniture to speak of was the table, which was surrounded by several solid-looking chairs. Maps of the city covered the walls, marks and designations on them I didn't know how to interpret. A lantern burned on the desk, shedding warm, dim light over the room.

The woman, Christine, stood as we entered. She wore a pair of faded black cargo pants and a beat-up tan tank top. Her hair was pulled back into a no-nonsense ponytail, and her eyes, framed by small wrinkles, were hard as glass.

"Christine, this is Lana Crow." Corin stepped aside to give the woman a clear view of me.

"Why isn't she restrained?"

My hackles went up at her brusque greeting, but I tried to keep my annoyance in check.

"We don't think she's a threat, Christine," Jae said quietly.

"You don't? From the report I received, it sounds like that's exactly what she is. Just because we haven't been able to find the connection doesn't mean she isn't working for the Representatives."

"She's Gifted, but up until today, she didn't know that. She has no allegiance to them."

Christine cocked an eyebrow at Jae, walking toward us. "The Blighted can be untrustworthy too; don't forget that."

She rested her hand casually on the hilt of the long, curved knife at her side as she stared at me. "Regardless of where she came from, she could still be a threat."

"*She,*" I snapped, my emotions flaring, "doesn't like being talked about like she's not here. And *she* doesn't plan on hurting anyone in this building."

Except maybe you.

The older woman's face hardened. "You broke into the home of one of my best operatives and tried to kill him. That's what I know about you right now. So don't ask me to trust you. The Representatives are getting smarter and smarter. They've finally realized we're a true threat, and I wouldn't put it past them to try to insert a sleeper agent in our ranks."

I bit my lip. I already didn't like this woman, but I couldn't argue with what she was saying.

"Then I don't know what you want from me," I said stiffly. "I can't prove I'm trustworthy. And I can't deny I tried to assassinate Akio. So if you're going to kill me, just do it already."

"No!"

The word was harsh and sudden, and I looked over at Jae, surprised at the outburst from the usually calm mage. He seemed as surprised as the rest of us were and quickly gathered himself, the neutral expression settling back over his face. "I'm sorry, Christine, but I can't allow that. I gave her my word she'd be safe. Her attempt on Akio's life failed, and she's offered us her help."

"Woah, wait!" I threw up a hand. "I haven't offered my help

yet. I agreed to meet with Christine, which I have. But so far, I honestly don't feel much inclined to help her with anything."

"You have no choice. I can't offer you leniency for your attack on Akio without some reassurance from you that you're on our side," she shot back.

My shoulders tensed. "I didn't even know there *was* a side until today! I hate the Gifted as much as anybody, but I don't like being forced to pledge allegiance to anyone or anything."

"This is a war, Ms. Crow. We have to make difficult decisions in the name of our cause. The only way to make absolutely certain you never attack one of my people again is to kill you. But if, as Jae says, you're one of the Gifted, maybe there's reason to keep you alive."

My throat tightened. This was too disgustingly similar to a conversation I'd had with the Gifted man, Edgar, years ago, when he forced me to leave my home in Wyoming to work for him. I'd spent years as his lackey, and even after he died, the mark he made on my life had remained. I'd never been able to go back to Wyoming, despite wanting to more than anything. Not as the person I'd become.

"I won't trade my freedom for my life," I said thickly. "You can kill me if you want, but you don't get to own me."

Turning on my heel, I strode quickly from the room, bracing myself for the attack that was sure to follow.

CHAPTER 9

No attack came.

I cleared the door in one piece, and my heart leapt as I dashed down the stairs. But it was too much to hope that Christine would let me leave here alive, despite the promises the men had made to keep me safe.

Sure enough, as I hit the bottom step, footsteps rang behind me. I darted across the abandoned factory floor, following a large assembly line belt, but before I got far, a hand grabbed my elbow. I yanked free and turned around, ready to fight for my life if I had to.

Warm brown eyes met mine as Fenris held his hands up in a gesture of peace. "Woah! Take it easy, killer."

"I won't stay here, Fenris!" I bit out. "She can't blackmail me into it!"

"I know, I know." He ran a hand through his dark, scruffy hair. "I'm sorry about that. Christine's tough, but she's had to deal with a lot. She's been burned too many times to trust people easily. And the circumstances of your arrival don't look great. Trying to kill Akio and all."

My shoulders sagged. "I almost didn't take the job. I hate assassinations. But I talked myself into it, thinking I was doing the world a favor—one less Touched man left to keep everyone else down. But what if..." I leaned against the cool metal side of the assembly line conveyor next to me, avoiding his gaze as I gave voice to the worry gnawing at me. "What if there were more like Akio? What if I was working against the Resistance without even knowing it?"

Fenris's expression softened as he stepped closer. "Then make up for it by helping us now." I started to open my mouth, but he overrode me. "*Not* because of what Christine said. Fuck her."

"Oh, really?" My eyebrows rose, and he grinned devilishly.

"Yeah. Don't tell her I said that though. She already thinks I'm insubordinate as it is. But really, fuck her. Don't join the Resistance because of her. Don't join because of me. Join us because you have a chance to make a difference here. I can't imagine what it's like to find out you're Gifted and never knew it. Must be a total mind fuck. But don't you see how that makes you the best ally the Resistance could ever have? You have all the power of the Gifted with none of the bigotry. You weren't raised in their world, so you can understand the Blighted."

A pigeon flew from the rafters, startling me. I watched it glide through the hazy light and disappear through a broken window before turning my attention back to Fenris. "What about Jae?"

"Eh, he's a special case. It took me a long time to trust him, but he's never let me down. He's talking to Christine right now. He'll set her straight. We need you, and I think she knows it. She's just not always great at asking for things instead of demanding them. Jae will make sure she understands how important you are. Even Akio told her he wouldn't let her harm you."

I snorted, pushing away from the conveyor belt. "Akio? Are you serious? The first thing I remember him saying when I woke up was 'can we kill her?' I find it a little hard to believe he'd do anything but dance on my grave if Christine decided to off me."

"Akio's all bark and no bite. And he's sensitive, like a delicate flower," Fenris added, pulling a laugh from me.

He beamed at my response and wrapped an arm around my shoulders. At five foot seven, I was no frail little thing, but Fenris had a good four inches on me, and I fit perfectly under his arm. He smelled of pine and citrus, a scent so intoxicating that for a moment I disobeyed all my old instincts and habits and slipped an arm around his waist, my other hand coming to rest on his stomach.

His muscles rippled under my touch, and I stepped back suddenly, coming to my senses. My usual policy when a guy I barely knew tried to touch me was "dick punch first, ask questions later." Why were all my usual defenses completely obliterated around these men?

"I do want to help," I admitted, clearing my throat. "If I'd known the Resistance existed, I'd have banged down the door ages ago offering to volunteer."

"See?" Fenris's deep voice was playful. "Everything happens for a reason. Come on. Let's go talk to Christine. I'm sure Akio's got her wrapped around his little finger by now. She can claim to be immune to his incubus wiles, but we all see right through that. Not that he'd ever use his true charm on her."

I suppressed a shiver. I hoped Fenris was right that the demon was lobbying to let me live. I'd heard about incubus and succubus charms, and how difficult it was to resist when they turned the full force of their allure on you. There was sexual attraction, yes, but out of that attraction came a desire to do anything it took to please them. And it worked without regard to gender or sexual orientation. A powerful incubus could charm anyone.

Feeling a bit like a petulant child who'd stormed off in a huff, I followed Fenris back toward Christine's office—or the "war room" as I'd heard him call it earlier.

When we walked in, Christine was sitting at the table, listening intently as Akio leaned toward her, speaking in low tones. She had a somewhat dazed, happy look on her face, and I wondered if Akio was really just using his "wiles" or if he'd boosted them a bit with some of his incubus charm.

When she saw me come in, the Resistance leader's gaze snapped back into focus, the hard look returning to her face. Akio stood back, his dark, inscrutable eyes settling on mine. The way he was looking at me now, I found it hard to believe he'd been advocating for Christine to let me live.

"Ms. Crow," Christine said, rising from behind the table. She leaned forward, her hands braced on the thick wood. Her knuckles were scarred and calloused, and I thought of what Fenris said about her having been through a lot. She looked about forty-five, maybe fifty, so she would've been my age now when the Great Death hit. I'd been so young when it happened I didn't remember the chaos and violence that erupted afterward, but I was sure they'd left permanent scars on her body and psyche.

"I've been told that my treatment of you may have been too harsh. As Jae and Akio have both pointed out, having another powerful mage on our side would be a huge asset. I admit they're right." She hesitated, as if she had to force the next words out. "I will not compel you to join our ranks, but rather ask you to. If you choose not to join us, there will be no punishment—although we *will* require a blood oath that you will no longer target any of our members, no matter the price put on their heads."

My eyebrows shot up. Akio had to have used his incubus charm to get her to make a concession that large. Or... did Jae possess some mind-control powers? I glanced at the mage, who stood to the left of the table, hands clasped.

A blood-oath was binding and could prove deadly to the person foolish enough to break it. But still, the fact that Christine was offering me an out was staggering. If I joined the ranks of the Resistance, I could do it knowing I was free and clear, that I was there of my own will, without a threat held over my head.

Fenris gave a light push on the small of my back, and I stepped forward. I tried to match her tone and bearing, feeling like I was standing in a court facing down a queen. I'd never been great at formalities, but this moment felt like it called for them.

"Thank you, Christine. That's very generous of you. But Fenris has convinced me that I owe it to myself to do what I know is right. I'd be honored to become a member of the Resistance and help in any way I can."

Christine nodded thoughtfully as she sat back down, leaning all the way back to kick her booted feet up onto the table. So much for formalities.

"I'm thrilled to hear it." Before I could breathe a sigh of relief, she added, "But I will need proof that you're as powerfully Gifted as you claim. What can you do?"

My stomach dropped. "I—I don't know."

The lantern light flickered off her eyes, making them glitter like jewels. "A mage who can't do magic is little help to us. Akio and Jae convinced me to spare you based on the merit of your talents. But what are they?"

This fucking bitch.

The temperature in the small, dingy office seemed to rise several degrees, but it was probably just my blood approaching the boiling point. Christine obviously didn't like being contradicted. Fenris was right; she was smart. Smart enough to listen to the advice given to her by men she clearly trusted, but also petty enough to make sure everyone in the room knew who was still in charge here.

I was tempted to storm out again and keep going this time, but Fenris's words had resonated within me. Not the "fuck Christine" part—well, okay, that too—but the part about turning the unsettling revelation that I had magic into a positive by using it for something good.

Gritting my teeth against the irritation building in my nerves, I felt around inside myself for that little spark of light—the magic that somehow lived within me. I could feel it, but I didn't have any idea what to do with it. How did I make it... go?

I tried leaning into my emotions, letting the tumultuous flurry of feelings rush through me. Jae had said my magic was agitated and reactive to my emotional state. Maybe I could force it out that way. And if it knocked Christine out in the process—hey, side bonus, right?

My heart rate sped up, my jaw clenched, and tears of anger and frustration pricked at my eyes.

But whatever magic existed inside me stayed dormant.

I could feel everyone in the room watching me, but I blocked them out, pulling and tugging on the flame inside me, trying to make it do something. The first time it had burst out of me, it happened entirely without my control. I hadn't even known it was magic.

The power burned steadily in my belly but refused to obey any of my commands. It was like a new limb I could feel but couldn't control. I wasn't even sure what muscles to flex. My body shook with effort, and sweat trickled down the small of my back.

Come on, you stupid fucking magic. Flare!

It stayed still and quiet, glowing softly in my mind's eye.

Gasping for breath, I bent over, heaving in big gulps of air. "I... can't."

Christine's voice was grim. "Then we have no use for you."

My shoulders slumped. I blinked rapidly as my hands curled into fists. I wanted to scream at the Resistance leader; it was incredibly unfair that although they had dozens, maybe even hundreds of Blighted members, I'd only be allowed to join their ranks if I could prove I was Gifted.

Smooth fingers pried open my clenched hand on the right side, and I glanced over, startled. Jae gave me a reassuring smile as he laced our fingers together, palms touching. Another hand reached for my left. Fenris gripped it tightly, his rough, calloused palm contrasting starkly with Jae's smooth one. I didn't know what they were doing, but I didn't try to pull away. Instead, I allowed the contact to anchor me, steadying my breath and my heartbeat.

A heavy hand fell on my shoulder, a figure appearing in my periphery. Corin.

I was trying to process my feelings about his wordless show of support, when Akio stepped up on my other side, his hand resting gently, hesitantly, on that shoulder.

Like a circuit being closed, power blazed through my body. The pilot flame burning inside me met with gasoline, and my whole body lit up. Now I could feel the magic filling my limbs, could feel it radiating from my body in winding tendrils. I focused it outward, directing it to latch onto the objects in the room.

Slowly, the boxes in the corner, the shelves, the table, and even Christine herself in her chair, began to rise off the ground.

CHAPTER 10

CHRISTINE SCRAMBLED to sit up straight, her legs slipping off the table. It was the same distance from the chair as it had been before, except now each piece of furniture floated about five inches off the ground, rising incrementally higher with every passing moment. Corin let out a murmured curse behind me, his grip on my shoulder tightening so much it hurt.

The Resistance leader was a tough old broad; I'd give her that. If someone levitated a chair I was sitting in, I'd have been out of that thing so fast there'd be nothing but a smoke trail left behind. But she just gripped the armrests and held on, her back rigid as a pole.

"All right." When that didn't get the response she wanted, Christine repeated the words more firmly. *"All. Right."*

I'd like to say I was just fucking with her at that point, but the honest truth was, I didn't know how to reverse what I'd done. The furniture still floated gently upward, almost a foot and a half off the floor now and continuing to rise.

"Jae...," I whispered out of the side of my mouth.

He gave my hand a gentle squeeze. "You can do it. Pull your magic back in—gently!" he added, as the table and chairs plummeted six inches, making Christine's knuckles go white.

Gritting my teeth, I tried to picture the tendrils of my power, imagining them wrapped around the furniture. Then I visualized drawing them back into myself, weakening and finally breaking the hold they had on the objects in the room.

It went... okay.

I actually felt a bit bad for Christine as her chair bounced and jostled, lowering slowly and unevenly back to the floor. When the legs finally hit solid ground, she remained seated, drawing in one long breath before addressing Jae.

"She's powerful, all right. But you'd better make sure she learns how to use her magic, or she'll be worse than useless; she'll be a danger to everyone here." She examined the group of us with a shrewd gaze. The four men hadn't relinquished their holds on me, and I still felt magic flowing through my veins like sap. "Since you four were so eager to bring her into the fold, I'm putting you *personally* in charge of training her— both magically and practically. Her successes and failures will be yours as well, so don't let me down."

She flipped open a box on the table and withdrew a half-smoked cigar. Clamping it in her mouth, she struck a match and gave a long pull. The tangy, sweet aroma lingering in the room intensified as she leaned back, putting her feet up again.

Two Blighted men walked in behind us, the taller one

knocking on the frame of the open door as they entered. Their booted feet froze in place as they took me in.

"Holy mother…," the shorter one, a young guy with bright red hair and a smattering of freckles across his face, whispered.

"Marcus, Dean." Christine waved them inside. Apparently, that was our cue to leave, because Jae gave my hand a gentle tug and the five of us turned toward the door. The two men stepped up to Christine's desk, rattling off a report about the movement of Gifted officials around the city. As we slipped out, she called after us, "I expect frequent progress reports. Take her to Akio's place until she's trained. And put a concealment spell on his house! I don't want any other assassination attempts."

I led the way down the rusty metal stairs. The high windows weren't boarded up, so the factory floor was much brighter than Christine's office had been.

"So, what now?" I slowed my pace when I realized I had no idea where I was going.

"We should take her to Asprix. He'll be able to get a read on her abilities," Fenris said from behind me.

"I agree," Jae murmured.

"Did you see Christine's face? It was fucking priceless. I can't wait to see what else you can do, killer!"

Fenris's confidence in my abilities made my chest puff up, and I turned around to grin at him, but stopped short when I saw the expressions on Akio and Corin's faces. Not everyone was as thrilled by my demonstration as Fenris was. Corin appeared unnerved and suspicious, and Akio's face was pinched in the same annoyed expression he'd worn almost nonstop since the moment I'd met him.

Jae stepped forward to lead us through the Resistance compound, and I fell into the center of the pack, my emotions vacillating between pride and self-disgust. I'd hated the Gifted my whole life, and now I was celebrating being one of them? I hadn't known what the magic inside me would do and hadn't meant to embarrass Christine by picking up her chair with her in it. But I couldn't deny I'd taken petty satisfaction in seeing her brought down a notch or two by my magic. Was this the slippery slope that came with being Gifted? How many steps were there between casually humiliating someone and using your power to oppress them?

My skin crawled, and for a moment, I wished I could dig the magic out of myself, open up a vein and let it pour out onto the dirty cement floor.

But it doesn't have to be that way. Look at Jae. Being Gifted doesn't have to dictate the kind of person I am.

The thought was only somewhat comforting, and I suddenly wished I were a better person to begin with. My lying, thieving, and bounty hunting hadn't seemed so bad when I thought of myself as just another tiny cog in the machine—someone whose actions couldn't have far reaching consequences. I'd felt so helpless that I leapt at any chance I could to take some of my power back, regardless of who it hurt.

"You okay?" Fenris nudged my shoulder as we walked, his brows scrunched.

"Yeah," I muttered. "Just... processing. What does this Asprix guy do?"

I had sudden visions of being strapped to a table, poked, and prodded while a wizened old man examined my magic.

"You'll find out soon enough. We're here."

We entered another large warehouse area. Except instead of cots laid out around the room, tables and chairs were gathered in clusters here. Around the perimeter, small kiosks were set up, with people cooking on small gas stoves or, in some cases, open flames. A few doors led to smaller side rooms, and the one we stopped in front of had a torn blue curtain draped across it.

Jae pulled aside the curtain, calling into the small room. "Asprix?"

"Oh, come in," a weathered, wispy voice responded.

We trooped inside, the four big men filling up the cramped space with their imposing presence. Little balls of light bobbed and floated across the ceiling, bumping into each other gently from time to time and changing course. They cast a cool glow over the room, highlighting the deep wrinkles in Asprix's face. He had white hair, which looked almost blue in the light, and a long beard that tapered to a dull point.

The space was small, with a cot and a crooked little table against one wall. The only other furniture in the place was the chair the old man sat in. When he saw who entered, his face split into a craggy grin, and he waved a bony hand. "Corin, my boy! How are you?"

Corin stepped forward, squatting down next to Asprix's

chair to look him in the eye. "I'm good, Asprix. How are you? You've been taking that tincture I had Val whip up for you, right? It should help your back."

Asprix patted Corin's cheek, shaking his head. "Sweet boy. Of course I have, though it tastes like an elephant's ass."

"That's how you know it's the good stuff. I'll bring you some more soon."

My heart clenched as I watched the two of them. The Corin kneeling down next to this old man, going out of his way to befriend him and take care of him—that was the Corin I knew. And when he talked to Asprix, the unfamiliar hardness in his face faded.

The old man looked up, taking in the rest of us, his eyes finally settling on me. "Ah. And who do we have here?"

"Lana Crow." I stepped forward and offered my hand, which he grasped gently in both of his trembling ones.

"Lovely name for a lovely girl."

I smiled at him, as Corin said, "Asprix, we need you to do a reading on Lana if you can. She... she didn't think she had magic, and now she's not sure where it's coming from."

"Oh my." The man's craggy face slackened as he looked at me again, more intently this time. "Ah. I see. Well, let me see what I can find out. May I have your hands, dear?"

He held out both of his, and I placed mine into them. As I did, I noticed that all of my fingers were bare.

My ring was missing.

I blinked. With the constant barrage of revelations and surprises since I woke up, I hadn't even registered its absence before now. Where could it be? Had it fallen off in my struggle with Akio? Had one of the men taken it while I was asleep? My eyes darted suspiciously around the group, but I kept my lips pressed shut. I didn't want to start an argument in front of this sweet old man.

Asprix's eyes clouded over, the light blue irises transforming to milky white as his eyelids fluttered like butterfly wings.

My palms grew warm, and a soft orange light filled the space between our hands.

"Oh my." Asprix's voice was faint, distracted. "So much power. It's a miracle it didn't kill you." His eyes shifted back to blue, and he looked at me sharply. "You just discovered your gifts?"

I nodded, deciding not to dispute his definition of the word "gifts."

"Well, they're not new. You've had magic all your life—powerful magic. But it's been repressed. Something was holding it back, and when that restraint broke, it was like a dam bursting."

Remembering the flash of blinding light that had erupted from me as I fought Akio, I shivered. *A dam bursting sounds about right.*

I hesitated, then admitted, "I used to have a ring. I had it as long as I can remember, and I wore it on the middle finger of my right hand. It's gone now. Could that have been the thing holding my magic in check?"

"Without being able to see it, I can't say for certain. But it's certainly possible. It would have to have been a powerful magic suppressant, but even that would lose strength over time." The old Gifted man's eyes went out of focus again, and the crease between his brows deepened. "Strange. Your magic is contained within you, but also held outside of you. It connects to…" He looked up, tilting his head to gaze up to the men who watched him as intently as I did. "To you."

"Who?" I bit my lip, both dreading and anticipating his answer.

"Them." Asprix's eyes cleared, excitement flushing his cheeks. "All of them."

"*What?*"

The word was on the tip of my tongue, but Akio was the one who voiced it.

"Her magic was suppressed for so long that when it finally burst to the surface, it was too powerful for a mortal vessel. So it reached out for anything it could find to stabilize it. You all absorbed a small piece of it, and she, in turn, absorbed some of your powers." Asprix looked at me with something like awe. "You, my dear, have powers linked to each of the men you've bonded to. Mage, shifter, and demon magic. All inside you."

"She didn't get anything from me," Corin said stiffly, still crouched beside us. I couldn't tell if he was disappointed or relieved by that fact.

Asprix let my hands drop and turned to pat Corin's head. "My sweet boy, she got the most important thing from you. Your humanity. Without you to ground her in the nonmagical, her powers would run rampant inside her, gnawing through her life-force like a hungry dog until nothing remained."

"I…" I wiped my sweaty palms on my pants, my thumb reaching over to twist the ring that was no longer there. "I don't understand."

Asprix beamed at me.

"It's quite simple, my dear. The five of you are magically bonded. Your essence entwined with theirs, and theirs with yours."

CHAPTER 11

THE ROOM WENT quiet as Asprix smiled up at all of us.

He was the only one who seemed happy about his pronouncement. Corin's face had drained of color; in the blue-white light, he looked like a ghost. Akio was muttering to himself in a language I couldn't understand. But I didn't need to know the words to get the gist of what he was saying, and it wasn't anything good. When I glanced behind me, Jae's face was thoughtful. And Fenris—

The wolf shifter picked me up and spun me around, making me squeak in a way that was neither dignified nor tough.

"I knew it!" he crowed. "I fucking knew it. This explains so much!" He set me down but kept his arms wrapped around me. I was too shocked to either struggle out of his grip or deck him in the face. He leaned back, his full lips stretching into a delighted smile. "I was going out of my mind wondering how I could've been mated to a Bligh—uh, not a wolf shifter. Ever since we woke up in Akio's kitchen after your magic surge knocked us all out, I haven't been able to get you out of my head."

"Of course you haven't," Akio growled. "Because every minute since she woke up has been consumed by *dealing* with her."

"Not like that!" Fenris insisted. "It's a... a pull." He shook his head. "Shit. I saw so many of my pack mates go through this when I was a little kid, but I didn't know it would feel like *this*." He swiveled his head, gawking at the others. "You guys don't feel that?"

Akio looked mutinous, Corin wouldn't meet my eyes, and I swore Jae blushed. And me? I was busy trying to make my new powers open a hole in the earth to swallow me up.

What I wouldn't admit, and planned to take to my grave at all costs, was that I knew exactly what Fenris was talking about. I'd wondered since the moment I woke up, in interactions I'd had with each of these men, why it felt like I knew them so well when I'd only just met them earlier today. With Corin, the connection had already been there, but there was absolutely no reason for me to feel comfortable with or trust the others. Yet I had.

I pushed Fenris's arms down and stepped back. He allowed me to break his grip but kept smiling wolfishly at me.

Dizziness flooded me, making my body sway. For a moment I feared I'd collapse onto Asprix, crushing him with my stunned dead weight.

"How do we... how do we break it?" I muttered through dry lips.

Fenris's face fell, a hurt look creeping into his eyes, and my heart twinged with guilt. But he had to know this was insane, right?

Asprix blinked, finally realizing the question was meant for him. "Oh. You don't."

I let gravity and the weakness of my legs pull me down to kneel beside him. Resting my hands on his knobby knees, I looked up at him with pleading eyes. "There has to be some way. Please. I can't—I don't—"

I shot a glance sideways.

Dammit. It was awkward as fuck doing this with the four men I was supposedly bonded to looking on. I wanted to ask for a moment alone with Asprix so I could explain to the sweet old man that his conclusion just wasn't possible, that he had to take it back somehow. That attachments were a weakness, and I could hardly bear the thought of letting one person into my life, let alone four. And that I wasn't the type of person who formed bonds anymore, magic be damned.

Licking my lips, I tried again. "I... I want to join the Resistance. I want to be part of this, and I want to learn to use my magic. But—"

"Ah, I'm sorry, my sweet. If you're hoping to break the bond between the five of you, I'm afraid to say that's quite impossible without destroying your magic, and most likely killing you in the process. And them."

My lungs seemed too small for all the air I needed right now. If it'd been just my own life at stake, I honestly would've considered risking it. But I couldn't take a chance with theirs like that.

Was that the bond talking? Or did I actually have a decent moral compass after all?

Grasping at another straw, I leaned closer to Asprix, speaking low in an attempt to keep this conversation private. Not that there was much hope of that. Sounds from the main room outside filtered through the thin curtain, but not enough to drown out my words.

"So, what? My magic is bonded to theirs, but what does that mean? Can we never be apart at all? Can I—"

"Leave their sides?" Asprix nodded kindly. "Of course you can. But I think you'll find you don't want to. And if you go too far for too long, you'll likely experience negative effects."

So I couldn't even take the coward's way out and run. My shoulders slumped, and I rested my forehead on the hands still clutching the old man's knees. His gnarled fingers patted my hair.

"I'm sorry to be the bearer of distressing news, my dear. But look on the bright side! Your magic is truly remarkable. Once you learn how to control and use it, you will be a force to be reckoned with. And who better to teach you how to use it than the men who share that magic with you?"

"Hell yeah! I'll help you learn to shift," Fenris volunteered.

Akio started muttering under his breath again. I could practically feel the anger radiating off him. Now that it had been given a name, I was uncomfortably aware of the bond I shared with each of them. The onslaught of their feelings jumbled up with mine, creating a riot of emotions inside my chest—not all of which I was certain were mine. Surely the thrill of happiness belonged to Fenris, not me.

Forcing my face into a neutral mask, I pushed to my feet. "Thank you, Asprix. At least now we know what we're dealing with."

"Anytime, my dove. Please come and see me again sometime. I'd love to find out how you all get on."

I didn't think I could respond to that in a polite way, so I held my tongue, stepping back to let one of the others take over. Corin shook his head, blinking slowly. "Yeah, thanks, Asprix. I'll bring you more of that tincture soon, okay?"

"You're too good to me." Asprix grasped his hand, his wise blue eyes studying Corin's strained face. "Ah, I see. An old wound. Old and deep." He clicked his tongue. "Nurture the seed of forgiveness, not resentment. Don't poison your bond, my boy."

Corin's head jerked back, and he shot me a glance seemingly against his will. Retrieving his hand from Asprix, he stood abruptly. "Let's go."

Without waiting to see if we followed, he pushed aside the curtain and strode out. Akio followed so close on his heels I was surprised he didn't trip over them. Corin's pace hardly slowed as we retraced our steps through the compound, into the guardroom, and through the dark maze of tunnels to the portal. In the abandoned house on the other side, dust plumed into the air as we all walked quickly through.

Even with our group spread out, I somehow ended up in the middle like always, with Corin and Akio ahead, and Jae and Fenris behind me. Not a word had been spoken among us since we left Asprix's small abode, which was fine by me.

By the time I reached Jae's flashy silver car, Corin was standing impatiently by the door, his hand hovering by the handle. Jae dispelled the wards, then pressed a button on the key fob as he came up beside me, and the car beeped, the locks springing open.

We piled inside, and a hush fell over the car.

"So... what do we do now?" Fenris asked. I'd felt his gaze on me the whole way back, and I could still feel it warming my skin.

"This doesn't change anything," Jae said. "Our directive from Christine is to train Lana and bring her up to speed. That's what we'll do. Akio, can we use your house?"

"Why not? Or what's left of it, anyway," the incubus muttered. He'd ended up in the front seat this time, forcing Corin to sit next to me.

Jae revved the engine and pulled away from the curb. This fancy, rumbly car was the loudest thing about him; it seemed an odd choice for the quiet, contemplative mage. Then again, we all had our guilty pleasures. Maybe one of his was flashy cars.

By the time we returned to Akio's place, my nerve endings were lit up with tension. The drive had been mostly silent, despite Fenris's best attempts to draw me into conversation. The sight of the destruction in Akio's living room and kitchen only seemed to ratchet the tension up another notch.

Akio, Jae, and Fenris gathered in the living room to discuss their plans for my training, and Corin suddenly seemed to take an intense interest in the art on Akio's walls. At a loss for what to do, I wandered into the kitchen. Broken dishes littered the floor and counters, mixed with spatters of blood. I picked up the biggest pieces and threw them away, then hunted down a broom in a little closet in the corner of the kitchen to sweep up the smaller shards. Once the debris was mostly cleared away, I went to work on the bloodstains. It was slow going; blood had slipped into the spaces between tiles, and it took some serious scrubbing to get the stains out. I was so absorbed in my task I didn't notice at first that the house had gone quiet. Finally, I looked up, realizing I had an audience. The four men stood at the edge of the kitchen tile, staring down at me as I kneeled on the floor with a rag in my hands.

"What?" I blew a strand of hair out of my eyes.

"What are you doing?" Akio's voice sounded strange.

I sat back on my heels, regarding them all carefully. "Look, I know this is all my fault. If I hadn't attacked Akio, none of you would have been around when my magic flared. You wouldn't have absorbed a piece of it, and we wouldn't be stuck together now. But we are. And I—somehow—have magic I need to learn how to control. I want your help. Magical bond or no, I need your help. And I promise to do what I can for the Resistance."

"But what are you *doing*?" Akio repeated, perfectly shaped eyebrows raised.

I looked down at the bucket of water and small pile of ceramic dust near me. "I'm trying to fix what I broke. I'll do the upstairs next. It'll take me a little longer to get to the hole in the wall. I don't really know what do to with plaster. But I'll clean up what I can." The incubus's eyes widened, and I raised a hand quickly. "All right, don't get too excited. You're not getting a live-in maid or anything. I only clean up messes *I* make."

"Too bad," Fenris murmured, his gaze hot. "You in a maid outfit...."

He trailed off, and I scrubbed a hand across my face to hide the flush creeping up my cheeks. As awkward as it was, I knew how to handle the other men's hesitancy and standoffishness. That was familiar territory for me, something I understood. Fenris's enthusiastic attention put me totally off-balance.

I cleared my throat. "Yeah, not gonna happen. Sorry."

He sighed wistfully, but I pretended not to hear it.

"We've discussed it and decided we'll each spend time with you, coaching you in how to use the magic you got from us. I've never taught spell casting to anyone but children, nor to anyone as powerful as you, so I'm not sure if the same techniques will work. We'll have to find the right access point for you to connect with the gift inside you. I'm going to pick up a few texts from my house that I think will help us. Your training will start tomorrow." Now that he was discussing magical theory, Jae's face lit up with excitement.

I nodded slowly. A lot of what he said didn't make much sense to me, but I assumed he knew what he was doing.

"We'll make this our home base for the time being," Jae continued, with a glance at Akio. The incubus's face darkened. "It'll draw less attention if we're all in one place and have fewer people coming and going. I need to go back to the Capital for a few days to put in an appearance with my family, but I'll put a concealment spell up before I go. Until we know for sure who wanted Akio dead, we need to play it safe."

The decision didn't shock me, though I thought longingly of my quiet, shitty little apartment in the Outskirts. Sure, the TV was always on, and a ghost hogged the couch. But it was mine.

"Yeah, okay." I squeezed the rag out over the bucket of water. It now had a vaguely pink tinge.

The men started to drift away, Fenris's eyes lingering on me as I resumed scrubbing. Probably imagining a damn French maid outfit.

"Hey, Akio!" I called before he disappeared up the stairs. He slowed reluctantly, then turned to face me.

"Yes?"

I cleared my throat. Apologies had never been my strong suit. "Look, I didn't *want* to kill you, okay? I know it doesn't make it better that I was doing it for money, but there was no ill will on my side. It was just a job."

"Right." His voice skated over my skin like a piece of ice.

I gritted my teeth, forcing down my own irritation. "I'm trying to say I'm sorry. No matter how we got here, we're stuck together now, so I don't want there to be bad blood between us." I tossed the rag into the bucket. Holding a piece of cloth covered in his blood while we talked probably wasn't helping this conversation go any more smoothly.

Akio's dark eyes glittered, scrutinizing me long enough to

make me shift uncomfortably. He opened his mouth as if to speak, then snapped it shut and vanished up the stairs.

I stared after him, a knot inexplicably twisting my stomach.

Well, I guess hate can bind two people as well as love.

CHAPTER 12

"You're still fighting it. Just *let* the change happen."

"I'm... trying," I ground out, baring my teeth as a trickle of sweat dripped down the side of my face. Maybe if I made my face as wolf-like as possible, it would somehow jumpstart my magic and force the shift.

"I know, killer. You're doing great," Fenris said encouragingly.

"How is she doing great?" Akio glanced up from where he was reading on the couch. The incubus had an amazing book collection. When—if—he decided to stop hating me, I'd ask him if I could borrow one. Or several. Unfortunately, that day wasn't likely to come anytime soon. His chiseled features were painted with disdain as he watched me crouch on the floor, attempting to shift into a wolf. "All she's done is sweat and complain. She hasn't shifted once."

Fenris shot him a quelling look. "She's trying. And that's *great.*"

Ugh. I did not need Fenris's fucking pity. Akio was right. I was failing miserably at this.

The guys had decided I'd learn to shift first; supposedly that was the easiest of my new skills to master, since it didn't involve controlling or directing magic, just letting magic flow through me to transform me. All I had to do was get out of the magic's way.

Apparently, my innate pigheadedness made that difficult.

I wiped the back of my arm across my forehead, puffing my cheeks and blowing out a breath.

"Good idea. Try less oxygen," Akio commented unhelpfully.

Dick. We'd see if he was still so smug when I turned into a wolf and bit him on the butt.

I shook my head, trying to dispel images of Akio's well-shaped ass clamped between my teeth. I'd never seen him dressed in anything that didn't perfectly showcase his body, from his broad shoulders to his trim hips and firm ass. Being physically attracted to someone I couldn't stand was extremely irritating. All my violent thoughts toward him invariably morphed into other kinds of fantasies, leaving me to hope no one noticed the blush spreading across my cheeks. I knew it was because he was a damned incubus—he was probably using his charm on me to torture me.

"Do you want me to get the other guys again?"

Fenris's voice wrenched my attention back to the lesson.

"No," I gasped. "I can do this."

I'd been working with Fenris on shifting for three days. The first day, we'd tried closing the loop like we had in

Christine's office, each of the men touching some part of me. It had unlocked my magic but hadn't helped with the shift. And I'd been terrified the whole time that I'd lose control and destroy Akio's house or something. Besides, I needed to learn how to access my powers on my own. Only being able to do magic when four men had their hands on me would be both awkward and horribly inconvenient.

"Fuck it!" Fenris exclaimed, making me jump. "I know what's missing! We need to get you out of this fucking sterile house."

"I'm assuming by 'sterile' you mean well-decorated and clean." Akio didn't even look up from his book. "In which case, thank you."

"Yeah, that's what I meant." Fenris rolled his eyes at me, and I stifled a chuckle. He sprang to his feet, hauling me up with him. "Hey, tell Jae I borrowed his car, okay?"

Akio muttered something that might've been an agreement as Fenris snatched Jae's keys off the counter that separated the kitchen from the living room. Since the house was now protected by a concealment charm and a protective spell, Jae hadn't bothered to put the wards up on his car.

The guys had insisted on bringing my Honda into the garage—not because it was worth protecting, but because it was too much of an eyesore. Leaving it on the street would draw attention. The incubus had seemed deeply traumatized by the sight of my shitty car in his spotless garage, which squashed any inclination I had to argue.

"Where are we going?" I asked as Fenris gunned the

engine, roaring down the street faster than Jae probably ever drove.

"Where wolves like to play the most." He shot me a killer grin, waggling his eyebrows. "The mountains."

I HAD NEVER WANTED to come to Denver, but the one thing I'd liked about the city right away was the stunning backdrop of mountains that rose up to the west. Having grown up on the plains of Wyoming, I'd been used to flat landscapes, so the mountains had always held a certain mysterious appeal to me.

But I had never actually been in them before.

The twitter of birds chirping in the distance and the crunch of dirt and rocks under our feet were the only sounds as we hiked up into the foothills. Tall, skinny pines rose up around us, interspersed with bushes and shrubs. Fenris had parked in a small turnoff at the base of the mountain, and now he led the way up into the wilderness.

"Is this where your pack used to live?" I asked, my voice shattering the peaceful silence.

He glanced back at me, looking pleased at my question. But a shadow crossed his face as he answered. "Near here. Our territory was a little farther south. I think a few lone wolves live there now. Most of them are in the city though."

"I can't see why anyone would want to live in the city when they could live here."

His rich laugh floated back to me. "Me neither. A lot of us don't have a choice though. It's hard for a wolf without a pack, especially in the wild. In the city, there are more ways to get by."

"You said a lot of shifters work as enforcement for the Gifted. Did you ever do that?"

A clearing opened up next to us, and Fenris diverted our course toward it. When we reached the small grassy area, he nodded. "Yeah, for a year. Worst fucking year of my life."

"I hear that." I grimaced, thinking of Edgar and the time I'd been forced into his service.

"It's amazing how the Gifted get us to work against each other, isn't it? Instead of attacking them?" His tone was serious, and I hesitated, surprised by both the insight of his statement and the depth of pain in his eyes.

"Yeah, it is. They took so much away from us, then gave us just enough back to make us feel like we're beholden to them."

"Yes!" The darkness in his eyes faded as he beamed at me. "That's exactly what I always say! See, we have so much in common."

I rolled my eyes. Fenris refused to give up on the insane idea that the bond between us was meant to be a mate bond. He'd mostly taken to joking about it or playfully pointing out our compatibility whenever the opportunity arose, but the expression on his face when I caught him gazing at me made it clear he still felt the pull as strongly as I did. But whereas the rest of the guys and I were perfectly content to ignore the bond, pretending it didn't exist, the wolf shifter seemed determined to embrace it with open arms.

"Yeah, yeah." I tried to brush him off. "Okay, so now that we're in the mountains, it'll be easier for me to shift?"

He grinned. "Actually, I have no idea. I just wanted to have you to myself for a bit. Plus, Akio was being a dick. That couldn't have been helping your focus."

I belted out a laugh. "Yeah, surprisingly, being heckled by an incubus doesn't make doing magic easier."

"Well, there are no incubi for miles up here. And who knows? Maybe being closer to nature *will* help."

"Okay. I'm ready."

He grabbed my hand and pulled me to the center of the small clearing. Sharp shadows danced on the ground as the afternoon sun cut through the trees around us. The air smelled of pine—just like Fenris always did. I inhaled deeply, loving the scent. After a moment, I kneeled and closed my eyes, finding the spark of magic burning in my center. Movement nearby ruffled my hair, and I felt Fenris crouch down beside me.

"Don't try to force it," he whispered, his husky voice raising goosebumps across the back of my neck. "Let it come. Imagine your natural form is a wolf. This form, the human one, *that's* the disguise."

The mountain air was cool on my skin, but I could feel sunlight on my face, warming every place the bright rays touched. I tried to imagine being a wolf in these mountains. Large paws thudding in an even beat against the ground as I raced through the wooded foothills. Tongue lolling and breath puffing in the air as I panted. The sound of other wolves calling to me before I answered them, head thrown back to howl at the sky. Heart racing as I hunted—

I gasped.

The dim light of magic inside me bloomed, expanding and filling my body like a river crashing through a ravine.

My bones shifted. It hurt like hell, but the pain was dampened by the surge of magic pumping through me. I felt my body change, my hands turning into paws, my face elongating into a snout, my tail wagging excitedly.

Holy. Fucking. Gods.

I had a tail!

I blinked, struck immediately by the way the world looked through these new eyes. My wolf eyes were sharper than my human ones, picking up small movements in the surrounding forest I would have missed completely before.

A cold nose pressed into my fur. *You did it, killer!*

Spinning in a circle, I caught sight of a large wolf. His fur was such a dark gray it was almost black, and he followed my body as I spun, keeping his nose buried in my white and red fur.

Good gods. You smell incredible.

I could hear Fenris's voice in my head, but more than that, I could clearly read his feelings. His happiness. His pride. His naked attraction.

My spine tingled in response, and I shook my fur out like —well, like a wolf.

I can't believe it. I did it! I ducked my head, circling around to sniff at Fenris. Oh, good gods. *He* smelled incredible.

Hey, thanks.

Dammit. I hadn't meant to think that "out loud." This mental link thing was going to be big trouble, I could tell.

Before Fenris could ferret out any other thoughts or

feelings I didn't want him to know about, I darted away, dipping my upper body low in a playful stance. He tensed, his amber eyes locked on me. We burst into motion at almost the same instant. I whirled, tearing through the underbrush, dodging over, around, and under fallen logs and bushes. Fenris ran hot on my heels, a howl bursting from his throat as he chased after me.

Even in wolf form, he was bigger than me, and he quickly overtook me, pulling up along my right side. I could barely keep my eyes on the terrain in front of me; they were drawn to the way his muscles shifted as he ran, the dappled sunlight glinting off his dark fur. He was so fucking beautiful.

He leapt onto a large boulder that rose up in front of us. Without even thinking, I leapt too, landing halfway up the rock and springing forward again almost as soon as my paws made contact. I reached the top, where Fenris waited for me. He tipped his head back and howled again, the sound so free and pure I wanted to laugh with wild joy. I threw my head back too, winding my howl around his in the cool mountain air. A flock of sparrows burst from a tree to our left, their tiny wings beating furiously.

Think you can beat me this time? Fenris's lolling tongue looked like a grin.

You're on, old man!

He leapt down the other side of the rock, leaving large paw prints in the earth. I followed as fast as I could, running with four legs as naturally as I'd ever run with two. I never stood a chance at beating him, but as we darted among the trees, I noticed Fenris easing up on his speed.

That fucker was taking it easy on me! Well, I'd show him what happened when he gave up his advantage.

Still slowing his pace, Fenris darted left around a thick pine trunk. I went right, and when we cleared the tree, I leapt for the dark gray wolf next to me, knocking him off his feet. We hit the ground together and rolled in a tangle of limbs and fur. He nipped at my ear when we came to a stop. His hot breath against my fur made my head fuzzy, and before I could think about what I was doing, I licked the side of his face.

Fenris's gold eyes—rimmed with the same deep brown they had in human form—flashed with heat.

My blood ran cold. Fuck. I had not meant to do that. I was supposed to be distracting him from thoughts like this, not encouraging them.

Not wanting him to read any of the thoughts in my head, I pulled desperately on the magic inside me, willing myself to shift back. Thankfully, it was much easier to return to human form than it had been to shift into a wolf.

Fenris sensed what I was doing and shifted along with me.

Unfortunately, we hadn't broken apart, so when the magic settled back down inside me, I found my human self straddling Fenris's much larger form.

Also unfortunately, I wasn't wearing any clothes.

The man beneath me had somehow managed to shift back fully dressed in his usual jeans, boots, and T-shirt, but I was naked as the day I was born.

A breeze hit parts of my body that should've felt no such thing, and I yelped, covering my breasts with both hands. If Fenris's eyes had been hot before, they were scorching now.

He reached up to grasp my hips, the pads of his fingers sending electric shocks racing through my body.

"Holy gods. You're fucking gorgeous, killer." His voice was rough and low.

"I'm naked!" I yelled, my voice sending another flock of birds scattering from a nearby tree.

He bit his lip. "Yeah, I noticed."

I gritted my teeth, trying to ignore the feel of his firm abs under my thighs and his grip tightening on the flesh of my hips. "Why am I naked?"

"Oh, uh, sometimes it takes a bit of practice to shift back wearing clothes."

"And you didn't think to mention that?" I hissed.

"Well, you're so powerful I thought maybe you could do it on your first try."

"Uh huh." I shook my head skeptically and batted his arms away before realizing what that left exposed. I quickly clamped my hands back on my chest. "Will you stop staring at me like that?"

"That's a tall order, beautiful," he murmured huskily.

"Close your eyes!"

Slowly and extremely reluctantly, Fenris dropped his eyelids. I braced my hands on his chest to scramble off his body, and he let out a low growl when I touched him. Wincing as sharp rocks and twigs that I'd barely felt as a wolf dug into my feet, I darted behind a tall pine tree, keeping a safe distance between its rough bark and my tender flesh. A sudden panic struck me, and I reached up to feel for the small quartz necklace I always wore. Still there, thank the gods.

"Clothes, please!" I called, holding a hand out around the trunk of the tree.

"Uh, sorry to tell you this, killer, but I don't actually keep a spare set on me."

I shook my hand adamantly. "Well, you'll figure something out. The birds and bees are getting quite a show here!"

A rumbling growl met my ears. Was he actually jealous of birds and bees seeing me naked? A moment later, he draped his large black T-shirt over my outstretched arm. I snatched it back and yanked it over my head. It covered everything—barely. The length was more indecent than the dresses the Gifted elite wore to those fancy clubs in the Capital. If I bent over even an inch or two, everything would be on display again.

"Pants!" I stuck my hand around the tree again and heard Fenris sigh in exasperation. "Hey, you dug this grave for yourself, buddy!" I called.

When he draped his pants over my arm, I tugged them on, tightening the belt enough to keep them on my hips. I stepped out from behind the tree and stopped dead.

Ah, fuck.

I'd overlooked the one major flaw in my brilliant plan. Now Fenris was nearly naked. He wore a pair of black boxer briefs, unlaced boots, and... that was it. The smooth planes of his chest and stomach were broken by a slight dusting of hair, and the V of his obliques peeked out from the dark fabric of his briefs.

When he caught sight of me, his full lips spread into a wicked grin.

"You look good in my clothes."

And you look good out of them.

I almost slapped a hand over my mouth as soon as the thought popped into my head. Thank all the gods he no longer had a direct line into my thoughts.

He quirked a brow. "Like what you see, huh?"

Then again, maybe he didn't need one.

I wrenched my gaze up from his sculpted abdominal muscles to his laughing eyes. He bent and started pulling off his boots, and I looked away from the delicious new view of his back muscles and impressive lats flexing and stretching.

"Um, what are you doing?"

"You're not gonna hike down this mountain barefoot, are you?" he asked, as if the answer was obvious.

"Neither are you!"

"Only got one pair of boots, killer. Sorry. Unless you want me to carry you? I do give a mean piggy-back."

My eyes shot back to him and I pursed my lips. "Do I look like the kind of woman who lets a man carry her around?"

He waggled the boot in his hand back and forth. "Well, that depends on the context."

"All right, give me that!" I darted forward gingerly and snatched the boot from his hand. He handed me the other, and I yanked them both on. My feet swam in the big shoes, but rocks and twigs no longer dug into my soles. "What are you going to do now, smart guy?"

A golden light spread over him. In another heartbeat, the dark gray wolf stood in front of me again. I hadn't realized how big he was when I was in wolf form too, but he was nearly as tall as my waist. His intelligent amber eyes gleamed.

This. I'll shift back when we get to the car.

The mental link between us was different when we weren't both in wolf form. I could still clearly hear his voice in my head, but I couldn't read his thoughts and emotions as easily as I had before. Thank the gods. Hopefully that went both ways and he couldn't peek into any of my uncensored thoughts either.

The gray wolf sniffed the air, then set off through the brush in a direction slightly different from the one we'd come from. I assumed he was taking us on a more direct path back to the car. I clomped after him in my too-big boots, slipping a bit on the twigs and stones that covered the dry ground.

It was surprisingly easy to talk to Fenris while he was in wolf form, and as we hiked down the mountain side by side, I told him about my love of books, my place in the Outskirts, and how I wondered if Ivy would even notice my extended absence as long as the TV still worked. I carefully avoided mentioning anything about my life before I'd come to Denver, or the mercenary work I'd done over the past several years.

He told me stories about growing up with his pack in the Rocky Mountains, and what a troublemaker he'd been as a pup. The happiness in his tone dimmed when he described what it was like living as a shifter kid on the streets of Denver. He'd lived in the Outskirts for several years until he got the job at Sparks, where Christine had found him. She'd kept him there for a while as an undercover operative, gathering information when he could. A lot of the privileged children of Gifted officials drank there, and alcohol loosened their lips.

I was almost sorry when we reached the car a couple hours later. The easy conversation had been nice; the last person I'd had any kind of long talk with was Ivy, and she'd been so distracted by the sitcom she was watching that all of her "uh-huhs" and "oh wows" were inserted in the wrong places.

The sun was low in the sky, and when Fenris shifted back to human form, it bathed his bare chest and scruffy face in a warm golden light. Shoving down the temptation to ogle him, I kept my eyes firmly on the scenery outside as we drove back in comfortable silence.

He pulled the car into Akio's garage, then hopped out quickly to open my door for me. I hesitated before accepting his hand, still not sure how to handle such chivalry. Who knew wolves had such good manners?

When we entered the house, Akio, Jae, and Corin were gathered around the kitchen bar, deep in conversation. They looked up as we entered, and then all three did a double take. I would've found it comical if my cheeks hadn't been on fire.

Akio glanced at Fenris's nearly naked form, then at me swimming in his large clothes. The incubus's lip curled, although I swore I saw a flash of heat enter his eyes.

"I take it you had a good lesson?"

Gods, kill me now.

CHAPTER 13

WARM LIGHT FILTERED in through the curtains, and I stretched languidly. I should get up, but it was hard to muster the motivation when the bed I lay in was so comfortable. Staying at Akio's house was like living in a five-star hotel—minus the friendly staff and mints on the pillows.

He had three guest bedrooms, and although I'd worried briefly that one of the guys would try to worm their way into my room, that possibility had never even been discussed. Corin and Fenris shared a room down the hall, while Jae stayed in the room downstairs. Jae had spent a few days in the Capital while I worked with Fenris, but he'd told me last night he had the next few days free. Now that I'd made a breakthrough in shifting, it was time to dive into spell casting.

My stomach roiled with nerves. Learning to shift had been difficult, though ultimately exhilarating, but I was genuinely scared to try performing spells. The few times magic had burst out of me, it hadn't gone well. And I still had a lingering distrust of magic users; part of my brain rebelled against becoming one of them.

Sighing, I flipped the covers off and rolled out of bed. Padding over to the closet, I perused the contents. I was running out of good options here. Akio had a disturbingly large collection of women's clothes—items left behind by years' worth of conquests—and I'd been raiding his "lost and found" bin for clothes since I hadn't had a chance to go back to my apartment.

I'd gone through most of the practical stuff already, and now I was entering the sluttier, skimpier portion of the wardrobe. I briefly considered asking Fenris if I could borrow more of his clothes, but I didn't think I could handle smelling like him for an entire day. Though the connection between us seemed to have strengthened during our time on the mountain, my resistance to it had strengthened in equal measure. The pull I felt toward him—toward them all—made me feel weak and vulnerable, and the self-preservation instinct that had kept me alive all these years worked hard to quash that weakness.

Pulling on a tight, low-cut black top and a pair of skinny jeans, I smoothed a hand over my wild red waves. Pretty soon I'd be wearing evening gowns around the house, unless I could convince them to let me go home and pack a bag.

I slipped out of my room and walked quietly toward the stairs. Fenris and Corin were probably still sleeping. The two of them were polar opposites of Jae and Akio, who were both ridiculously early risers.

My heart clenched at the thought of Corin. I kept trying to

find a moment to talk to him in private, but every time an opportunity arose, he'd find some excuse to leave the room. He had to take a call from Christine, or deal with a Resistance emergency, or... *anything* but speak to me. And if I was being honest with myself, part of me was relieved. I knew we needed to talk, but the enormity of the things I needed to say froze me in terror.

Akio's living room was bright and spare, the hardwood floor cool under my bare feet. The only blemish on the pristine sight was the crater in the plaster by the door, which still hadn't been fixed. Maybe Jae could teach me how to do it with magic—though home repairs were just about the most boring use of spell casting I could think of.

The mage looked up from his seat at the kitchen bar when I entered, his long, graceful fingers lifting a mug of steaming liquid to his mouth. I doubted it was coffee. Jae didn't have any vices or guilty pleasures as far as I could tell, except maybe the expensive cars thing. As I stepped closer, the vaguely spicy aroma of some kind of tea hit my nose.

"You're up early," he noted, intelligent green eyes watching me carefully. They flickered down for just a second toward the annoyingly ample cleavage this top displayed, but his expression remained neutral.

"Early is relative. Compared to those two lazybones down the hall from me, yeah, I'm up early. But I have a feeling you've got me beat by at least an hour." I slipped onto a chair across from him, trying to calm the rapid thrumming of my heart.

It's just magic, Lana. Not a firing squad.

Jae dipped his head to acknowledge the truth of my words. "Are you ready to get started?"

I swallowed. "Yeah, sure. As I'll ever be."

"Good. Come with me."

We headed down the hall to Akio's office. When we stepped inside, my mouth fell open. I'd never been in this room before, and now I wasn't sure I ever wanted to leave. Three of the four walls were covered with large bookcases, and tomes of all colors and sizes filled the shelves. I knew Akio was an avid reader, but I hadn't realized his collection was this amazing.

I stepped past Jae, running my fingers over the spines of the books, as if I could absorb everything in their pages just by touching them.

"You like to read?" His voice was soft and warm.

"I love it."

"That's good. That will be a great help as you study magic."

"It will?" I turned to him, surprised.

He nodded, green eyes serious. "Some of the Gifted can only do one kind of magic. Elementalists, for example, can control one or more of the elements. Witches and warlocks can brew potions, but their power ends there. Wizards have magic inside them, but can't access it without complex incantations. Powerful mages, however, are limited only by their ability to keep learning."

Two chairs sat against the wall with no bookshelves, a small table between them. Jae took a seat, and I followed him dutifully, curious despite my apprehension.

"I knew mages could get really powerful. Are there any

who know all the magic there is to know?" I asked, settling in the chair opposite him.

He shook his head, his elegant features softening. "You're looking at it the wrong way. There are endless possibilities in spell casting. Magic is just the building block, the raw material to be shaped by your will. Or not shaped. If you don't learn to control it, it will run rampant. This is why most mages start training at a very young age. Control is paramount in magic."

The way he was describing my powers, as an almost separate entity that existed inside me, made me cringe.

He went on. "I'm in the minority in this opinion, but I also believe it's imperative for mages to study history and philosophy. We wield great power, and too many mages treat that power as a right rather than a responsibility. They learn how to tame their magic, but not how to tame their own natures."

I cocked my head at him curiously, not quite sure what he was getting at.

He pulled his chair away from the wall to face me more fully and leaned forward, resting his elbows on his knees. "Have you ever had a bad day, Lana?"

I snorted a laugh. "Tons of times."

A slight smile lifted the corner of his delicate lips, before he said, "So have I. Have you ever been so angry or frustrated that you lashed out at someone or something you shouldn't have?"

Ugh. Way too often. I dipped my head in a nod, suddenly self-conscious about my quick temper.

"So have I," Jae assured me, though I had a very hard time

believing that. Without realizing it, I'd mirrored his pose, leaning toward him as he talked. His brilliant green eyes held lighter specks that seemed to glitter in the morning light, and I felt myself falling into their depths as he continued. "Now imagine that instead of just lashing out with your fists or words, you had the power of the universe at your fingertips. What kind of spells might you cast in anger?"

I gulped. That thought was terrifying.

"That's how too many mages live. They've learned *how* best to use their magic, but not *why* or *when*. The capacity for empathy and self-discipline becomes exponentially more important the more power one has."

That made sense. But gods, if I felt nervous about being Gifted before, I was sweating buckets now. "Jae, I—"

He took one of my hands gently, his smooth fingers tracing a soft pattern over my palm. "I don't know you well, Lana. But I believe you're a good person and one completely worthy of the magic you have. But I would be remiss if I started teaching you spell casting without reminding you of the implications of the power you wield." Jae's eyes darkened, the beautiful green retreating as his pupils dilated. "I take care to control my emotions, to let my higher instincts rule my baser ones. I've seen too many mages corrupted by power, and I've witnessed the pain it can cause."

He paused for a moment, staring at the patterned rug on the hardwood floor, lost in his own thoughts.

My brows furrowed. It seemed more like he'd *experienced* the pain it caused. But before I could press him for more information, his face cleared, the peaceful demeanor returning.

"But that having been said, it's time for you to learn some magic. Let's start with levitating, since you seem to have a penchant for it."

His lips tilted again in an almost-smile. I had a feeling he would have a great sense of humor if he ever let it out. Whether because of his magical training or whatever it was in his past that had hurt him, he seemed determined to tamp down any extreme emotions—even the positive ones.

I had a sudden desire to draw him out, to break past his calm facade and see what the man behind it was really like. Blinking, I shook off the thought. I should be more concerned with controlling my own wild impulses than trying to draw wildness out of Jae. The words "cool" and "collected" had never, ever been used to describe my temperament. But if I wanted to use my magic without risking the safety of those around me, I was going to have to try.

"Okay." I grinned. "I wonder how mad Akio will be if I make his desk float?"

TURNED OUT, Akio did *not* like it when I made his furniture levitate.

He never would have found out if I hadn't lost control as I was lowering it back down, but the heavy thud drew all three of the other men in the house racing to the study. He ranted and raved about "respecting other people's property" while I tried to suppress my grin of satisfaction. Drawing on my magic without being connected to the four of them was vastly more difficult than it was when we were touching, but I was slowly learning how to spark the power on my own.

After that, the incubus forbade us from using his study for any more of our lessons, so for the next few days, Jae and I were relegated to practicing in the living room. We hadn't done any more levitation, but he'd taught me an illusion spell I could use to make myself invisible. That one had been harder to learn, but I had been *extremely* motivated. As someone who made her living sneaking around, the power of invisibility was almost too good to be true.

Unfortunately, Christine had called shortly after the desk incident and informed Corin that the Resistance made a strike on a shipment of food and other goods bound for the Capital. All operatives were to lay low until further notice since the Peacekeepers would be out in force looking for the culprits.

Our living situation had felt crowded enough before, but now that none of us could leave, it felt positively stifling. Four men, one woman, and a million confusing emotions were too much for one house. To avoid Fenris's hot glances, Corin's stilted silence, and Akio's grousing, I threw myself into my studies with Jae.

The mage was unlike any other Gifted man I'd ever met. In my experience, most of them were power-hungry, self-involved assholes, but Jae was the complete opposite. He was thoughtful, careful, and empathetic. Being in his presence was a balm on my soul, his placid green eyes soothing my turbulent emotions. We spent half our time together practicing spells and the other half just talking, discussing philosophical ideas and concepts of morality I found fascinating.

Jae was obviously smarter and better educated than I was, but he never made me feel stupid, listening carefully to my thoughts and opinions and responding with interest. Akio always cocked an ear to listen in on our conversations, though he pretended not to. But Fenris and Corin's eyes glazed over when they heard us, Fenris's tongue lolling out of his mouth like a dog on a hot day.

But at the moment, all four men were focused intently on me.

And I was focused on my empty palm, which hovered just in front of my face.

The room was silent except for my slow, even breaths.

"You know… this would be… a lot easier… without an audience," I said, careful to keep my emotions from burbling up.

Stay focused, Lana. You control the magic; it doesn't control you.

"Yeah, but we don't want to miss the big moment!"

Fenris's body was nearly vibrating with excitement. His belief in me both bolstered my confidence and terrified me. This was hard enough when the only person I would let down if I failed was myself.

"And it's important you learn how to do magic with distractions present. Combat spells in particular will almost never be cast in an ideal, quiet environment. You need to be able to find your focus even in the midst of chaos."

Despite his words, Jae's voice was soft and soothing. Maybe tomorrow he'd make me do this spell while winging plates at my head, but for today, I could tell he just wanted me to succeed.

I closed my eyes for a second, stoking the banked energy of magic inside me and relaxing my muscles to let it flow through me. Then I lifted my lids and stared intently at the empty space above my palm.

Three heartbeats later, a small flame burst into existence, hovering a few inches above my hand.

"Ah ha!" My eyes widened, and I glanced quickly over at the guys, afraid if I took my gaze off the flame for more than a second, it would disappear. But it kept burning, steady and strong, a tiny little ball of magical fire.

Fenris let out a whoop, and Jae clapped his hands together.

"Holy gods! I did it!" I stared at the fireball for a moment longer, studying the hypnotic detail of the shifting orange flame, and then curled my hand into a fist under it, dispelling the magic.

"Well done, Lana." Jae's green eyes shone with pride. "Now see if you can do it again."

My confidence bolstered, I held out my palm once more, drawing on the magic inside me. When I latched onto it, I directed it toward my hand and—

The wall of Akio's house exploded.

CHAPTER 14

THE BLAST HURLED ALL five of us across the room. Pieces of wood pelted me like shrapnel, and I shook my head to clear it as I staggered to my feet.

Adrenaline roared through my body, panic rising in my throat like bile. "Oh, fuck! Jae, I didn't mean to—"

"That wasn't you, killer," Fenris said grimly. All four men stepped in front of me, forming a protective barrier. "That came from outside."

I looked toward the destroyed front wall of Akio's house. The dent in the plaster that I'd been determined to fix one day no longer existed. The gaping hole near the door was choked with dust and smoke, but through the haze, I could see several figures approaching.

"But... what about the wards? The concealment spell?"

Jae raised his hand as he answered, a spark of blue flame flaring above his fingertips. "They must have a ward stripper. But I don't know how they broke through the concealment. They shouldn't have been able to, damn it."

He shook his head in frustration, but Fenris nudged him. "We can worry about that later. First, let's not get dead."

My mind cleared, the initial wave of panic subsiding as my body prepared for a fight. This, at least, was familiar. I reached down and ripped away the bottom half of the stupid dress I'd been stuck wearing this morning, revealing the twin dagger sheaths strapped around my thighs.

Akio glanced back at me, his dark eyes widening as they slid down my body. "Is this really the time to—?"

"It's so I can fight, jackass. Don't look if you don't want to see anything."

Before he could respond, Jae threw out his arms and hurled a blast of blue fire at the approaching figures. The one in front, a wiry man with a nose that looked like it'd been broken at least twice, gestured quickly, and a wall of ice sprang up in front of them. Jae's magic slammed into it, sending cracks skittering across the surface of the ice.

"They have an elementalist," he said grimly. "I'll deal with him. You three, keep Lana safe."

I bristled at that. I'd keep myself safe, thank you very much. Or if not safe, I'd at least take a few of these attackers out with me. I'd never been one to sit out a fight. To drive that point home, I jostled my way forward just as Jae shot another ball of flame at the wall. The ice shattered, revealing five figures behind it, and my dagger flew through the air a second later, impaling the tallest one in the chest. He grunted and dropped to his knees, then toppled forward like a felled tree.

Fenris shot me a wide-eyed look. "Holy fuck, killer! Look at you."

I shrugged deprecatingly, but my chest swelled. Damn right. Unfortunately, there was no time to bask in the radiance of his beaming smile. As soon as their buddy went down, the other intruders rushed forward, pouring through the hole in Akio's wall. They were all dressed the same, I realized—in the blue and gray uniforms of Peacekeepers. Shit.

The elementalist hurled an ice spear at us, and our group split as we all dove away from the projectile. I tucked into a roll and hopped back to my feet, rising just as Jae did.

"I've got the elementalist." Jae's brown hair was mussed, but his voice was steady. Even in the midst of battle, he kept a tight lid on his emotions. He gestured, sending a ball of fire hurtling toward the man. The elementalist met it with a blast of water. The two forces met with a hiss, and steam erupted into the air, obscuring my vision again.

Somewhere across the room, a loud growl sounded. Fenris must've shifted. An answering roar shook the room, and through the haze, I could make out another large animal form. A mountain lion met Fenris's wolf in a clash of snapping teeth and bared claws, and my throat tightened with worry. I ran forward, but before I could reach them, something struck the ground in front of me and another explosion erupted, knocking me off my feet. I flew sideways, twisting in midair to look over at my attacker. A woman with hair so blonde it was almost white drew another potion out of a belt around her waist.

I pulled the second dagger from my thigh sheath and

threw it at her. The blade sliced across her forearm, and she shrieked, dropping the vial of potion she held. It exploded as soon as it touched the ground, throwing her backward. I scrambled to my feet, my eyes locked on hers as she rose. The witch's lip curled back in an angry snarl, and she launched herself forward, sprinting toward me as she reached for her belt again.

Fuck. No more daggers left.

I reached for my magic, stoking the flame of power inside myself. Jae must've been right about my penchant for levitating things, because without thinking, that's what I did to the witch. Her forward motion was arrested as she rose into the air, her legs continuing to flail furiously, but her feet no longer gaining any traction. Before she could chuck another potion, I darted forward, aiming a roundhouse kick at the side of her body. She flew sideways, hitting one of the intact sidewalls and sliding down it. I dove after her, nailing her with a wicked punch to the face. As her jaw went slack and she slumped over, I yanked off her potion belt, fisting it in one hand. I didn't know what any of these little vials did, but I was sure they were more powerful than my own current magical offerings.

Jae and the elementalist were still trading blasts of blue fire and ice. Corin and Akio fought off a gray demon that moved with superhuman speed. Between the two of them, they were keeping him occupied, but neither of them seemed to be able to land a punch on him. He was too damn fast.

"Corin!" I screamed.

He grunted as the demon landed a blow to his ribs, and

when it turned to do the same to Akio, he took advantage of its distraction to shoot a glance at me.

Years ago, in what felt like another life, Corin and I had come up with a series of simple hand gestures we used to communicate during jobs. I still remembered every single one, and I prayed he did too. I made the gesture for *take cover,* then threw a vial filled with dark iridescent liquid their way. Corin grabbed Akio, diving out of the way as the potion landed at the gray demon's feet.

The glass shattered, and liquid slithered up the demon's leg like some kind of possessed snake. He howled in agony, clutching at his leg. He moved with lightning speed, but the liquid moved with him, crawling higher up his leg and eating away at the flesh.

Corin helped Akio to his feet as they watched the gray demon move erratically around the room, screeching and trying to scrape the black liquid off his skin.

"Thanks," Corin panted.

I nodded, my gaze darting around the room. Fenris and the mountain lion shifter still circled each other, but the mountain lion had a large gash in its beige fur and was breathing heavily. Jae drove the elementalist into a corner, pummeling him with blasts of blue light.

I looked around again. "Wait, weren't there five? Where's the fi—"

A cracking sound rent the air, and a glowing whip flew toward me, wrapping around my upper body.

"He's invisible!" Corin cried, racing toward the seemingly empty space where the whip originated.

A glowing white lash with three tails snapped out, catching him across the arms and torso. He grunted and fell back, streaks of red blooming across his chest. The magic rope binding me hauled me forward. I struggled, trying to loosen its hold on me, but the thing was like a fucking straightjacket. I couldn't get a good windup with my arms pinned, but I twisted my whole body and threw the belt with the potions toward the invisible figure, hoping something would break and do some damage.

A white thread of magic whipped out, wrapping around the belt before it even hit the ground. The figure began to coalesce. Corin had been wrong; it was a woman. She was petite, with dark hair that floated around her head like she was channeling a thousand volts of electricity. Each of her hands held a glowing white whip, one of which was still pulling me forward.

Strong arms wrapped around me from behind, holding me back. The dark-haired woman snarled, yanking harder.

"Let her go."

The voice speaking near my ear was Akio's, but… not. It was smooth as velvet, decadent as fine wine. The dark-haired mage's eyes widened, and she shook her head as if to clear it.

"Release her now. I'm sure we can think of better things to do than fight. Wouldn't you agree?"

The incubus's deep voice was liquid sex, full of a promise so tempting that, even though he wasn't addressing me, I unconsciously craned my head to gaze up at him, my body pressing back into his. I couldn't catch my breath, and all I wanted was to drown in his scent.

Our faces were mere inches apart. Glancing down at me, Akio dropped a small kiss on my nose, and that slight touch banished every thought from my mind. My body felt like it was floating, weightless and heavy with lust at the same time.

The mage seemed to be swaying on her feet a bit too. Turning his attention back to her, Akio slipped out from behind me, stepping forward and grasping the taut magic rope. He used it to reel the mage in closer to him. She stumbled forward until he caught her, wrapping his arms around her. Her whole body shuddered, and a sudden flash of jealousy ripped through me even as the bind constraining me loosened.

Corin darted forward, unwinding the glowing magic whip from around me. I stepped back, attention still locked on Akio and the female mage. Her eyes were hooded, her hair twisting above her head like charmed snakes while Akio brushed his lips against the shell of her ear, whispering words too low for me to hear.

Finally, he stepped away. The mage remained where she was, eyes unfocused and hands idly tracing paths up and down her body. Her magical whips had vanished.

"The charm won't hold her long; she's strong. We need to get out of here." Akio turned to us, looking over my shoulder to address Corin. It was just as well. I didn't think I could meet his eyes right now. My cheeks flushed with embarrassment as the lust in my mind cleared.

Corin grabbed my hand, pulling me toward the garage. "Guys! We gotta go! *Now!*"

Fenris leapt after us, leaving the body of the mountain lion shifter behind. His gray snout was covered in blood.

The elementalist threw an ice spear to intercept us, and we ducked. It crashed into the kitchen cabinets, shattering wood and porcelain. Jae took advantage of the man's momentary distraction to launch a fireball at him. The elementalist turned too late and was engulfed in flames. He screamed, dousing the fire with water as the sickening smell of burnt flesh filled my nostrils.

We poured into the garage, heading for Jae's sleek silver car.

Before Jae could unlock it, the car filled with water, which turned immediately to ice. A sheet of ice formed on the outside too, sealing the doors closed.

The elementalist braced himself in the doorway, sagging weakly, half his hair burnt off but a look of triumph on his face.

"Mine! Mine!" I wrenched the door of my shitty Honda open, flipping the visor down to grab the keys.

Everyone piled inside as Jae sent a scorching blast of flame toward the elementalist. The man's magic must have been tapped out, because no water doused the flame this time. He fell back into the house as the doorframe caught fire, the blaze catching quickly. I slammed the car into reverse, the old gears screeching as I cranked the wheel. I was about to peel out down the street, when Jae put a hand on my arm.

"Wait," he said softly, looking back toward the house. A flicker of fire glowed from inside the garage, and smoke was beginning to fill the space. He looked into the back seat, catching Akio's eye.

"Do it." The incubus's voice was grim.

Jae closed his eyes. I couldn't tell what he was doing, but I felt magic pouring from him.

The house shook, rocking on its foundation as if a magnitude eight earthquake tore through the earth just below it. The wall with a hole in it was the first to go, buckling under the pressure. Before it collapsed entirely, I saw the mage with the electric whips still standing where we'd left her, arms limp by her sides. Then the falling rubble obscured her as the rest of the house came down with a thunderous crash.

I stared at the pile of plaster, wood, and stone where Akio's house had once been, my jaw dropping.

Holy shit. Jae had just destroyed Akio's house.

And Akio had let him.

I was stunned, both by the raw power Jae had displayed and Akio's sacrifice. No one inside could've survived that collapse, which meant there was no one to report back to whoever had sent them. True, his house had been fairly well trashed in the fight anyway—thank the gods it wasn't all my fault this time—but he'd just lost everything. All his fancy-ass clothes. All his *books*.

Twisting in my seat, I shot a look back at the incubus, wanting to say something.

His dark eyes were cold.

"What are you waiting for?" he barked. "Go!"

Gulping, I threw the car into gear and tore off down the

street, clenching my jaw on my sharp retort. Whatever warmth I thought I'd seen in his eyes earlier had obviously been an effect of his incubus charm.

"Damn it, this car is a fucking magnet for Peacekeepers," I muttered, keeping my eyes peeled for any sign of a lurking officer. Even if they had no idea we were involved in the fracas at Akio's house, my old beater stood out in this neighborhood like a neon sign.

"I'll put an illusion on your car. Nothing flashy. Just enough not to draw attention." Jae's focus was glued to the rearview mirror.

I drove aimlessly though the streets of the Capital, trying to stay away from heavily trafficked areas.

"Where are we going?" When I was sure we weren't being followed, I glanced back, taking in the rest of the car. Corin was sitting in the seat behind me, and the amount of blood soaking his shirt made my stomach drop.

"We need to get back to the Resistance headquarters," Jae said grimly. "I'll guide you."

Silence settled over the car, interrupted occasionally by Jae calling out a new direction. We passed through the gate to the Outskirts without incident, and I slowly began to recognize our surroundings.

When we pulled up alongside the old house that hid the portal we'd gone though before, I hit the brakes harder than I meant to, jerking everyone forward in their seats.

All that was left of the house was a smoldering shell.

CHAPTER 15

"WHAT THE FUCK?" Fenris breathed, leaning across Akio to stare out the window.

Jae got out of the car, scanning the street warily. I did the same but could see no movement. The neighborhood was long since abandoned, and it looked like whoever had started the blaze hadn't stuck around.

Leaving the others behind, we crept into the burnt-out remains of the house. The roof was gone, and chunks of charred wood littered the floor. Jae picked his way over to the basement, sending up a ball of glowing light to hover a foot above us like a lantern. The stairs looked too damaged to trust, but Jae darted down them anyway. I followed, stepping as quickly and lightly as I could. The place where the portal had been was nothing more than a black burn mark, the edges glowing red like embers.

Jae ran his fingers over the glow, his brow creased. "They

tried to break into the portal. They didn't get through, but the portal is destroyed."

I studied his face in the darkness. The dim light hovering over us cast his features in harsh shadows. "Is that good or bad?"

"Both. The portal did what it was supposed to do by keeping intruders out. But now we need to get to another portal quickly—and hope that one is still intact."

We hurried back up the stairs. I stumbled when one of the planks snapped beneath my foot, and Jae reached back to catch my arm, pulling me onto the relatively stable main floor.

When we got back in the car, Jae filled the others in on the state of the portal downstairs before murmuring directions that would take us to an alternate entrance to the Resistance.

"Shit." Fenris rested his hands on our headrests as I drove, leaning forward. He was stuck in the middle seat between Corin and Akio, the three large men squashed together. His stormy gaze darted between me and Jae. "This can't be a coincidence, right? The attack on Akio's place, the portal getting destroyed. The Representatives must be closing in."

"I don't want to speculate until we talk to Christine." Jae's hand tightened into a fist on the middle console, before he added, "But I don't believe in coincidences. Corin, were you able to reach Christine?"

"No. Phone was on the couch. It got left behind." Corin's voice was tight with pain, and I winced in sympathy. I'd gotten a few lumps and bruises, but he'd taken three brutal lashes across his chest. I pressed harder on the gas, careening through another decrepit pocket of the Outskirts.

An agonizing twenty minutes later, Jae directed me to stop in front of a tall, redbrick building, then led us up the stairs and into a supply closet halfway down the hall on the third floor. We stepped through the portal there, appearing in the dark, labyrinthine basement of the abandoned factory where the Resistance was headquartered. Jae conjured another ball of light above us, and we walked quickly through the tunnels. When we reached the guardroom, four people greeted us instead of the two there had been last time—three men and a woman, and none of them were sitting or playing cards. They stood alert and tense, and as soon as they saw us, they all reached for their weapons.

"We were attacked." Corin stepped forward, his voice commanding despite its weakness. "We need to see Christine immediately."

I noticed that Jae hung back behind the rest of the group. It made sense. Even though the mage was obviously committed to the Resistance's cause, I was sure some people here still didn't trust him. Or me, based on the looks they were shooting my way.

But the desperation radiating from us, and the blood soaking Corin's shirt, seemed to convince them he was telling the truth. The four guards stepped away from the door, letting us pass through. As soon as we entered the main compound, Corin staggered, sucking in a pained breath and raising a hand to the gashes on his chest. I slipped under his arm, draping it over my shoulders and turning to Jae.

"These cuts need to be taken care of right now. Which way to the barracks?"

He inclined his head left, and I tugged Corin in the direction he indicated.

"I'll report to Christine." Fenris darted off the other way.

When we reached the room full of cots, I found an empty one and lowered Corin onto it. His eyes were half closed, his face tight with pain. I pushed him onto his back gently, tearing open the front of his shirt to examine his wounds.

I bit my lip. Fuck. They were deeper than I'd thought. The skin had split open cleanly, almost down to the bone in places.

"Do you have a healer here?" I asked Jae.

He knelt down beside me. "No healer. But I know a bit of the healing arts. I can teach you. It's a skill you should have."

Godsdamn it. I would've much preferred to sit back and let Jae handle this. But he was right. What if one of them got injured in the future and he wasn't around? I'd hate myself if I couldn't help them because I'd been too scared to learn how.

"Can I?" I asked Corin softly.

His eyes were screwed up, and I wasn't sure if he was really paying attention, but I wouldn't make him my healing guinea pig without his go-ahead. There was enough resentment lingering between us already; I didn't want to betray his trust again.

He nodded once, gritting his teeth. I looked to Jae, waiting for instruction.

"This is a spell where empathy becomes very important," he said softly, hovering his hands above Corin's chest. I did the same, placing my hands next to Jae's. Our fingers brushed, the contact soothing me. My heartbeat slowed a bit, and I managed to draw in a steady breath, gathering my focus.

"Okay. I'm ready."

"Find the magic inside you and direct it outward. But at first, don't try to *do* anything with it. Just feel." Jae's voice was soft in my ear.

I followed his directions, reaching out with my magic like it was a sixth sense or an insect's antennae, trying to gather information about what was in front of me. Instead of closing my eyes, I focused on Corin's clear blue ones, using that connection to help my magic find what it sought.

Finally, I latched onto it. I could feel Corin's essence, feel the thrum of life flowing through his body. And I could feel the interruption of that life in the deep gashes across his chest.

Not daring to speak, I nodded my head slowly.

"When you're sure you have a grasp on the injury, pour magic into that gap in his life force. Let it knit him back together," Jae murmured.

I clenched my jaw, fear rising to the surface. What if I poured the wrong kind of magic into Corin and ended up hurting him instead of healing him? Was that possible?

No. It's Corin. You won't hurt him. You won't let yourself.

Focusing on that thought, on how I'd do anything to keep him safe and happy, I slowly began to stoke the fire of my magic. He sighed deeply, but it wasn't a pained sound. After a moment, his wounds began to close. Jae removed his hands from beside mine and rose, standing behind me and gripping my shoulder as I kneeled over Corin. The contact bolstered my magic, and I kept feeding it into Corin's wounds until the skin closed over completely.

Pulling my gaze from the deep blue pools of his irises, I checked my handiwork. His chest was still covered in blood, but the three gashes now looked like very fresh scars, pink and shiny.

Jae's hand slipped off my shoulder as I wiped a trembling arm across my forehead, scrubbing away the beads of sweat that had gathered there as I concentrated.

"Are you okay?"

Corin rose up onto his elbows, shifting slightly as if to test the pliability of his newly formed skin. "Good as new."

I snorted. "Yeah, that's what you said after you got kicked by a buffalo on your first hunt. But I seem to remember you needed fourteen stitches."

"Twelve." He swung his legs over the side of the cot, setting them gingerly on the floor. His torn shirt hung off his shoulders like a very unfashionable vest, and I used the fabric to wipe some of the blood off his chest, trying not to notice how familiar the lines of his body were. His lean waist, his firm stomach, the scar under his left collarbone that had required—

"*Fourteen* stitches," I insisted, poking at the old scar playfully.

Corin huffed a laugh. "I guess I should take your word for it. You were the one who patched me up."

"Like you'd rather have had Margie do it?" I arched an eyebrow in challenge.

"No. I wanted you."

His eyes met mine again, open and vulnerable for the first time since I'd met this new version of Corin. My hand on his chest stilled, the bloodstained fabric of his shirt slipping from my grip.

As if realizing what he was doing, Corin stiffened, straightening. His eyes closed off again, their clear blue color just as beautiful but nowhere near as inviting. He broke our gaze, glancing down at the piece of quartz strung around my neck on a thin leather string.

"Why do you still wear that?"

His voice was blunt, not angry or bitter, just—blank. And the lack of emotion cracked my heart open. If Jae and Akio hadn't been standing nearby watching our exchange, I'd have let the tears stinging my eyes pour down my cheeks. Hell, maybe I would anyway.

"Because you gave it to me. I've always worn it," I whispered. "I'll never take it off."

Corin reached out, gently running a finger over the smooth stone. His skin barely touched mine, but I shivered at the contact.

"Why did you leave, Lana? With no word, no warning, nothing. You were just… gone."

I braced my hands on the edge of the cot on either side of him, still kneeling at his feet. "I had to, Corin. Edgar, he would've—"

"Would've what? Whatever he did, we could have survived it together. Whatever your life has been for the past eight years, it could've been *our* life."

"But Margie—"

"We could've figured it out," he insisted. "Made something

work. We were stronger together, and we should've stayed that way."

One rebel tear tracked down my face. "You always said that. But sometimes the only way to be safe is to be apart."

Corin shook his head, huffing out a breath, then drew his hand back and leaned away. He regarded me silently for another moment before turning to his two teammates who stood like sentinels behind me.

I rose on shaky legs to join them. I hadn't meant to start this conversation here, and I knew it was far from over. But we had other problems to deal with at the moment.

"Sorry about your house, Akio," Corin said wearily.

"It's fine." The incubus's voice was dry. "It was just... my house."

"That's plenty. I can't—"

"You!"

The harsh cry interrupted Corin's response, and we all whipped our heads around to see Christine striding toward us with a heavy gait. Fenris trailed behind her, his expression worried.

The Resistance leader raised a shaking finger to point at me. "You! How long have you been working for the Representatives?"

CHAPTER 16

BEFORE I COULD BLINK, Akio, Jae, and Corin were before me, separating me from Christine. As the furious woman reached us, Fenris slipped from behind her to join the rest of the men.

I craned my neck, trying to see over or through the wall of muscle in front of me, as Jae asked, "What's going on, Christine?"

"This *Gifted*"—she spat the word—"is a mole for the government. She's betrayed us."

"You accused her of working with them before, but as we pointed out then, if the work she did as a mercenary benefitted the Representatives, she was unaware of it. She's pledged herself to the Resistance, and I have no reason to doubt her."

"You have no reason to doubt her?" Christine snapped. "Of course you don't. You're all infatuated with her." She glared at me over Akio's shoulder. "The Representatives chose well, I'll give them that. Red hair, pretty eyes, a perfect sob story, and she managed to seduce not just one, but four of my best operatives!"

My face flushed, both in anger at the accusation and embarrassment at her describing my connection with the four men in such crass terms. I was sure from the outside it looked just as she'd described. I hadn't known any of them except Corin for longer than two weeks, and yet we'd become undeniably close.

"Hang the fuck on, Christine. That's not fair." Corin's broad back flexed with tension, and his voice was hard.

"Fair is irrelevant. Your little spy is endangering all of us, even if you're too blind to see it!"

Sick of being talked about in the third person—and itching to land a punch on Christine's face—I pushed my way between Akio and Jae, meeting the Resistance leader's glower.

"What exactly are you accusing me of, Christine? I've spent the last week training with these men so I can help the Resistance, and I gotta tell you, it really fucking pisses me off to be accused of subterfuge when I've given up everything to join your cause." I gestured to both sides, indicating the state the five of us were in. Corin had been injured the worst, but we were all banged up. "In case you missed it, we just got attacked by a bunch of Peacekeepers!"

Her nostrils flared. "I know you did. You weren't the only ones."

"*What?*" Corin shared a grim look with his teammates.

"You four, war room. Now." Christine jerked her chin in my direction. "Bring her."

She turned on her heel and stalked off. Four sets of eyes

turned to me, and I met their gazes defiantly, expecting to see suspicion and anger in them. To my shock, I saw no such thing. Not even from Akio.

"I didn't do it. I didn't betray the Resistance," I said staunchly.

"We know that, killer. But we need to find out what's going on. Will you come?" Fenris held out a hand.

The trust in his eyes made my chest ache. I wasn't used to having people believe me. Christine's reaction, as harsh as it was, was more along the lines of what I'd grown to expect from people. I knew the Resistance leader didn't like me, and I didn't like her much either, although we both supposedly served the same cause. But I trusted the men not to let her find me guilty of a betrayal I didn't commit.

Nodding, I slipped my hand into his.

The barracks had quieted with Christine's arrival, everyone riveted to the scene playing out before them. Faces that had been cautious and closed off were now openly wary or hostile, and I wished Christine hadn't leveled her accusations against me in such a public setting. The Blighted had decades' worth of reasons not to trust the Gifted. Now they had one more.

As we made our way to the war room, the men fell into the same unconscious flanking pattern they always did. Fenris kept a firm grip on my hand—the stubborn, independent part of me told me I should pull away, but I couldn't bring myself to do it—while Jae fell into step on my left side, and the other two walked close behind us. But I didn't feel like a prisoner being escorted.

I felt like a queen being guarded.

There were a few Resistance members I didn't recognize gathered in the war room, heads bent low over a map laid out on the large table. Christine stood next to them, arms crossed over her chest.

Her head snapped up as soon as we entered, and she gestured to a chair in the corner next to a stack of crates. "Put her over there. Bind her."

"We're not going to do that, Christine. You have presented us with no actual evidence that Lana is a traitor. We're here to listen and discuss. That's all." Jae's voice was calm and firm, but his magic pulsed in powerful waves.

I was sure everyone in the room could feel it, and I wondered if he was doing it on purpose to intimidate the human Resistance members, or if he didn't have as firm a grasp on his emotions right now as he usually did.

Christine's jaw muscles twitched. "Fine. But watch her. And keep her out of the way." She shifted her body to block my view of the map on the table, pointing toward the corner where the lone chair sat. Grudgingly, I walked over and plunked down onto it. Fenris went with me, never letting go of my hand. Christine noticed that connection and scowled as the other three men approached the table.

I couldn't make out any part of the map from here, but I could see their faces as they leaned over to look at it. Corin's eyes widened, and Akio cursed softly.

"You see it?" Christine asked, a note of triumph in her voice.

"Yeah," Corin breathed, his expression anxious.

"These are all the houses that were hit?" Jae studied the large map intently.

"Yes. All the attacks occurred within an hour of each other. You see the pattern, don't you?" Christine pressed.

"They form a perimeter around the Resistance's location."

"Exactly." Christine tossed a glare over her shoulder at me. "Some of the houses hit belonged to Blighted civilians, not connected to the Resistance at all. Several belonged to our people. There were three casualties on our side and more injured. No prisoners taken, thank the gods. But you see how all the attacks are clustered around us? Someone is using a tracking charm to find our location. And they're getting closer."

My mind swam, trying to process what she was saying. I had no idea where the Resistance was actually based; I'd only ever come here through portals, and Jae said he moved those every few weeks to keep the Gifted government from being able to detect patterns of movement. For all I knew, our actual location was miles from the redbrick building we'd entered earlier.

I tugged on Fenris's hand, and he leaned down toward me.

"Doesn't Jae have some sort of concealment spell on this place?" I whispered.

He nodded grimly, eyes focused on the group gathered around the table as he answered in a low voice. "Yeah, he does. One other low-level mage helps him maintain it. But this is a big place. It's hard to keep it totally concealed. What his spell really does is keep people from finding our hideout if they don't already know where it is. They could walk by it twenty times and never notice it. But if a tracking spell is leading them here... well, it'll still be hard to find, but on the fifth or sixth time passing by, they won't overlook it anymore. That's probably why the attacks were clustered around our location. The Representatives don't know quite where we are yet, but they have an idea of the general area. They'll keep testing and poking, following whatever tracking spell they have, until they break through the concealment."

Fuck.

"I don't know any tracking spells! I didn't know any magic at all until eight days ago!" I called to Christine, though my mind was racing. If the Representatives were closing in on the Resistance location, that meant *someone* in the organization was a mole. And that was a problem.

Her steely eyes met mine. "Yes, Ms. Crow. I remember you telling me that story. But I have no way to verify it and no reason to believe you."

"There are two attacks that don't fit this pattern, Christine." Jae hovered his graceful fingers over the map. He looked up. "One is Akio's house. He's in the Capital, miles away from here. The other is the attack on the portal at the building on Field Street. It was burned out, the portal destroyed. That's an anomaly in this pattern as well."

"You're right." Christine drummed her fingers on the tabletop. "But they do fit another pattern." She turned to face me fully this time, head tipped back as she stared down her nose at me. "They're both places your new friend Lana Crow has visited."

CHAPTER 17

I SURGED TO MY FEET, dropping Fenris's hand. He caught my elbow instead, holding me back from charging at Christine.

"I didn't fucking do it! I'm not running a godsdamned tracking charm!" I shouted.

"This place is more than just the headquarters for the Resistance. Did you know that?" The older woman regarded me evenly. "This is also a haven for those unjustly persecuted by the Gifted. We have families living here, hiding from death sentences leveled against them for crimes as minor as scavenging from a restaurant's discarded scraps in the Capital. I hope you realize your actions have endangered those people along with the active Resistance fighters."

I pressed my lips together, thinking of the hundreds of cots and blankets spread out in the barracks. All those people at risk....

"Then you should be trying to strengthen the concealment spell, figure out how the government is *actually* tracking the location, bolstering defenses—I don't know, something! Something besides wasting time leveling baseless accusations at me just because you hate me."

Jae had been studying the map carefully, his elegant brow furrowed. Now he looked up at me, his face grave. "Lana... it is possible."

The air left the room.

It must have, because I suddenly couldn't breathe.

My world tilted on its axis, leaving my head spinning. Jae didn't, *couldn't*, believe that. He couldn't believe I'd betray the Resistance, betray the four men who had come to mean so much to me.

It hurt more than I would've thought possible to think I had lost his trust.

"No," I said weakly. "I swear, I didn't—"

"It's possible," he repeated, stepping closer. "That you've been tracking us and didn't even know it."

I blinked. "What?"

"I believe you when you say you were unaware of this. And I know you don't know any tracking spells. But it's still possible you're carrying one."

My stomach lurched. The relief of knowing Jae trusted me was nearly overshadowed by the new fear creeping over me. "Carrying one?"

He sighed, turning to Christine. "We need to take her to Asprix right away. When we had him read her magic, we didn't have him scan her for any external charms. An oversight on my part, and I take full responsibility. But it didn't even occur to me that she could be carrying a tracking spell. She was sent to kill Akio, after all. Whoever hired her had no reason to think she'd end up joining us."

Christine tipped her head, glowering at me. I could practically see the gears turning in her head. Even if Jae convinced her it wasn't intentional on my part, I was certain she'd never forgive me if it turned out I was the one who'd drawn the Representatives' attention to the Resistance base.

Finally, she nodded curtly. "Do it. Report your findings back to me immediately."

Fenris's grip on my elbow had shifted from one of restraint to one of support, as my legs had grown weak. Now he gently ushered me toward the door, where the other three men met us. I followed them down the stairs numbly. When Corin pushed aside the curtain to Asprix's little room, my blood chilled at the sight of the old man. He could give us answers, but I wasn't sure I really wanted to know them.

Unaware of my inner turmoil, the white-bearded reader's face lit up at the sight of us.

"Corin! It's good to see you again, my boy! And you brought your friends with you, I see." Asprix's gaze fell on me, and the joy in his light blue eyes dimmed. "Are you quite all right, my dear?"

I shook my head, attempted a smile, and drew in a choked breath all at the same time. It was a confusing mix of signals, the sum of which probably gave him a clearer answer than words ever could.

No.

Fuck no.

"Oh dear." The wizened old man tsked through his teeth. "Well, what can I do for you?"

"We need you to read her again, Asprix. But instead of focusing on her own magic, see if you can uncover any evidence of an external spell placed on her. Specifically, a tracking spell," Jae said.

Asprix's eyes widened. "Oh my! Yes, of course. If I may, my sweet?"

He held his wrinkled hands out like he had the last time. Forcing my body into motion, I knelt before him and rested my hands on his. A white film clouded his eyes, which almost seemed to glow in the light from the tiny glowing orbs that bounced and jostled against each other on the ceiling.

I gnawed my lower lip while he worked. He was in his trance for so long I was afraid I'd end up eating a chunk of my lip. I could taste blood by the time he finally blinked, his eyes clearing.

"Well?" I blurted.

Asprix pulled his hands back and sat straighter in his chair. Feeling suddenly cold, my fingers twisted around each other, my thumb reaching over to nervously spin the ring on my middle finger—the ring that was no longer there.

"I didn't even notice it before," he said softly, and my heart sank.

"So... I am being tracked?"

"I'm afraid so, my dear. It's a small charm, very discreet. Not terribly powerful, but quite sophisticated. Whoever created it is quite skilled."

The back of my neck prickled as a wave of nausea washed

over me. Edgar, the Gifted man who'd blackmailed me into leaving Wyoming and working for him in this damn city, had branded me with a tracking charm on my nape, just below my hairline. I'd lived with that brand, along with the knowledge that he could always find me, for years. It had faded out after his death, the spell no longer having anything to connect to. But I swore I could still feel it sometimes.

Had someone reactivated it somehow? Was that even possible?

"Fuck." Fenris gave a low whistle. "Trouble really does find you, doesn't it, killer?"

He softened his words by stroking my hair gently, and I reached up to cling to his hand, gaze still focused on Asprix.

"Can you tell who put the tracking spell on me? Or when?"

Asprix ran his knobby fingers through his beard. "No, unfortunately. I do know that whoever created it is still alive. But I can't tell you more than that. Can you think of any Gifted people you had contact with recently who would have reason to track you?" He hesitated for a moment, considering. "Although I suppose it would be possible for them to create a charm that could be applied by a third party. So you may never have even met the true caster of this spell."

My jaw dropped.

Well, that narrows it done a whole fucking bunch, doesn't it?

"So, it could be… anybody," I choked out.

Asprix's wrinkled face drooped as he confirmed my fear. "Yes. I'm sorry, my dear."

"Well, that narrows it down a whole fucking lot, doesn't it?" Fenris swore, and I looked up sharply. Was our shifter mind-connection growing stronger even in human form? Or were we just that much alike?

Either way, we were both right. The endless possibilities of who could've created the spell made tracking down the source virtually impossible. I thought I'd done a pretty good job staying under the radar, but I was beginning to realize the government was watching the Blighted population more closely than I'd thought.

"We need to tell Christine about this," Jae said softly.

"Are you kidding me?" Corin rounded on him. He'd ditched his bloody shirt sometime on the way to Asprix's room, and his muscles were bunched with tension. "If we tell Christine she's carrying a tracking spell, she'll never believe Lana didn't do it on purpose!"

"We have to tell her," Jae repeated. "If we don't find the origin of that tracking spell, whoever is behind it *will* find us. There are lives at stake." Corin opened his mouth again, his eyes blazing, but Jae raised a hand. "I will let her kill me before I let her kill Lana. But Christine needs to know."

I tried not to hear the words *I will let her kill me before I let her kill Lana.* They were too much for my overloaded brain to process right now. I could no longer deny the connection that bonded the five of us on what felt like a soul level, but such a naked admission of it made my heart hammer with unfamiliar emotions.

Corin's hands clenched by his sides. "You're right. Fuck, you're right. But we're not bringing Lana back to the war room until we calm Christine down. I want her to *guarantee* Lana's safety."

Jae nodded solemnly. "Agreed."

Akio turned to Asprix, who was watching the entire exchange with sharp eyes. "Can we leave Lana in your care for a while?"

I bristled, his words shocking me out of my stunned state. "Hey! I'm not a fucking baby."

His dark eyes glittered as they perused my body. "I've noticed."

Glancing down, I took in my appearance. Christine had barely blinked when she saw me, so I'd almost forgotten I was still wearing the top half of a deep green evening gown. I'd ripped off the bottom half at my upper thighs, and my empty dagger sheaths were still wrapped around each leg.

"Hey, I told you. If you don't want to see anything, don't look."

"And I heard you," he said, his lips tilting into a rare smile, his gaze still pointedly glued to me.

I lapsed into silence, unsure how to reply. Was he actually joking around with me? This was one of the least antagonistic exchanges Akio and I had ever had, and I was afraid if I opened my mouth again, I'd ruin it.

Fortunately, I was saved from having to formulate a response when Asprix spoke up. "Of course she can wait with me! We'll get to know each other a bit better. Won't we, dear?" He rubbed his hands together, looking excited at the prospect.

Well, at least one person in the Resistance—besides my four—didn't hate me.

"Thanks, Asprix." Corin patted the old man's shoulder.

"Be good, killer," Fenris added, winking at me as they

disappeared through the curtain separating Asprix's cubby from the main room.

I stared after them for a moment, trying to gather my thoughts.

"Are you all right, dear?"

A laugh burbled out before I could stop it. "As good as a newly made Gifted woman who just discovered she unwittingly betrayed the only people she's ever truly belonged with can be. Thanks for asking."

Asprix gave a watery chuckle. "Well, certainly none of those four believe you betrayed them."

"It doesn't matter though, does it? The plain truth is that however this damn tracking charm got put on me, it's leading the authorities right to us." A thought struck me, and I turned to face the old reader. "They hit Akio's house and a portal location I'd visited before. So does that mean the tracker is sending signals from everywhere I've been? Like a... trail?"

He nodded, stuffing a small pillow behind his head and leaning back. "Very likely, yes."

I was suddenly doubly grateful for the day Fenris and I had spent running around the foothills in wolf form. Let whoever was tracking me waste time trying to follow *that* path.

"But the strongest signal will probably come from wherever you currently are," Asprix added.

Sliding down the wall next to his chair, I propped my forearms on my knees and rested my head against them. My current location was the one I most feared the Representatives discovering.

I couldn't stop thinking about what Christine had said,

about how this place was a haven for those in need as well as the seat of the rebellion. Her story about the Blighted families hiding out here had struck home. I knew plenty of other people who had run afoul of the Peacekeepers but hadn't been lucky enough to escape. If the families who'd found safety here were discovered now, hiding out with a group of rebels, their punishment would be a thousand times worse. The Representatives would use them as an example, not caring what their actual crimes were.

"Don't worry, dear." Asprix looked down at me kindly. "It will all be all right."

His eyes drooped tiredly, and I wondered for the first time how old he actually was.

Old enough that he should be living out his days in a comfortable house with big windows and curtains that flutter in the breeze, not this stuffy little cubby lit only by magic.

"Thanks, Asprix." I didn't believe him for a second, but arguing with him felt mean. If he still had some hope, I wasn't going to take that away from him, even if I couldn't share it.

A few minutes passed.

Then a few more.

After several more minutes passed, I lost track of exactly how long I'd been waiting, but I was leaning toward calling it "forever." And with every second that ticked by, the vise of fear and anxiety tightened around my heart.

What was taking the guys so long? Was Christine unwilling to believe I hadn't intentionally led the Representatives here? Had there been more attacks in the surrounding area? Were Gifted enforcement agents gathering outside even now?

Finally, I turned to Asprix, intending to ask him if tracking spells could be physically removed—I was willing to lose some blood, or maybe even a limb, if it meant getting this damn thing out of me—but stopped when I saw the old man's head lolling, his face slack with sleep.

I watched his chest rise and fall gently, an all-too-familiar sick feeling tightening my stomach.

Whoever was hunting for the Resistance headquarters was attempting to find it through me. I couldn't undo the damage that was already done, but I could make their job a little harder.

I could leave.

CHAPTER 18

As soon as the thought passed through my mind, my entire body chilled, as if someone had thrown a bucket of ice water over me.

I didn't want to leave.

Though I'd only been a member of the Resistance for a short while, it was the first time in my life I felt such a strong sense of belonging and purpose, as if this was what I was born to do.

But it was that exact same sense of purpose urging me to leave now, to protect the people here at all costs. And to protect the group of men who had burst into my life with the force of an exploding bomb, changing everything I thought I knew about myself and the world. Until I could figure out a way to remove this tracking charm, I was a hazard to everyone around me. Staying here, continuing to put the Resistance base in more danger than I already had, just because I *wanted* to, was selfish and small.

Rubbing my arms to banish the goose bumps creeping over my skin, I glanced over at Asprix. His mouth hung open slightly. He looked peaceful in sleep, and I hoped the men wouldn't be too hard on him for letting me slip away.

Corin will despise you forever if you go, a voice whispered in the back of my head. I shoved it down. If he and the others were safe, his hatred was a price I was willing to pay. But I had to move quickly, before they returned from their talks with Christine.

I scrunched my eyes shut and reached for the magic burning low inside me. The high emotions ricocheting through my body made concentrating difficult, and it took several deep breaths before I was able to relax enough to let the power flow through me. Then, just like I'd practiced with Jae, I envisioned myself in my mind's eye and scrubbed gently at the image, as if rubbing out a pencil sketch with an eraser. When I was finally satisfied, I opened my eyes and blinked down at myself.

My body looked just the same as it had before.

I wasn't sure why I even bothered to check. Jae had explained that illusion and invisibility spells didn't appear to the caster, only to outside observers. My mind was the one that created the illusion, so it couldn't be fooled. Unfortunately, that meant there was no way for me to tell if the spell had actually taken effect.

Gods, I hope it worked.

Not wanting to waste another second, I stood and nudged the curtain aside, peering into the main room. People were spread throughout the large space, talking and eating, but no one glanced my way. I slipped out, careful to avoid bumping into a short, stocky woman who walked past. Her gaze slid right through me, and I breathed a silent sigh of relief. Jae was a good teacher.

I found the guardroom near the entrance easily and hovered outside, waiting for an opportunity. After a few minutes, a large blond man pushed through the door, a woman with a long brown braid wrapped around her head following him. Before the door swung closed behind them, I darted through it.

Inside the entry room, the four Blighted guards settled back into a watchful stillness. I held my breath as I tiptoed across the room.

"What is it, Bronwen?" A male voice behind me made me freeze.

"I can still feel the magic from that Gifted woman. Gives me the creeps."

"Yeah, me too. Don't know why Christine let her in here. I don't trust her one bit."

"Eh, I dunno," a third voice piped in. "The other one's not so bad. Hell, if they can help us, why not—"

I didn't wait to hear the rest, slipping into the dark tunnel leading to the portals. Navigating the passages without the aid of Jae's light was difficult, and I wasted another few minutes agonizing between two portals, trying to decide which was the one we'd come through. They all looked the same to me. Finally, I stepped through the one on the left, breathing a sigh of relief when I recognized the supply closet.

I let the invisibility spell fade as I hustled down the stairs.

Outside the tall brick building, I yanked open my car's passenger door and popped open the glove box, then rooted around inside. My hand finally closed on what I sought—a small glass cylinder. My last transport spell. I'd kept it in my car in case I ever got pulled over by Peacekeepers and things went south.

Setting it on the ground, I lifted my heel and stomped down sharply, shattering the cylinder. Purple smoke billowed out, enveloping me in a hazy cloud.

As the smoked cleared, the familiar dingy walls of my apartment came into view. The TV was on, blaring a magical reality show at an unbelievable volume as Ivy watched raptly. Good gods, it was a miracle my neighbors hadn't broken down the door and stormed the place.

"Ivy! Volume! Please!"

I had to shout over the sound of the television, and the ghost's translucent head whipped toward me.

"Lana! You're back!" Her face lit up as she clapped her hands lightly.

Deciding not to wait for her to attempt to lower the volume with her incorporeal fingers, I darted forward and snatched up the remote, mashing the button down until I could hear myself think again.

Ivy watched me the entire time, and as I tossed the remote back down on the couch, she said, "You look different."

I sighed, running a hand over my half dress. "Yeah, well, my wardrobe selection got a little slim."

She kneeled on the couch, leaning over the back to get a

closer look at me. "No, that's not what I mean. You're... glowing."

My eyebrows shot up. Had something gone wrong with my invisibility spell? I thought I'd let it drop, but maybe I'd somehow gone too far the other way and added a glow to myself? I glanced down at my body but didn't see anything out of the ordinary.

"No, I'm not."

"Yes, you are!" she insisted, pointing to my belly. "It's strongest right there, but it spreads all over you."

Oh. She was talking about my magic. She could see it.

I walked around the couch and sat next to her, leaning back and letting my body sink into the lumpy, springy cushions. "Um, it's been a long couple of weeks. A few things have changed, and this glow is one of them."

Ivy nodded thoughtfully, brushing a strand of her sleek blonde bob back into place. "Is another one how sad you are?"

I tilted my head to look at her. "What?"

"You seem very sad. You don't look good, if I'm being honest."

"Hey!" I batted at her, making sure not to let my hand actually pass through her. It wouldn't hurt her, but touching a ghost always gave me the chills.

"Not like that!" She leaned back, as if trying to get a more complete picture of me. "Although you don't look good in that way either. But you look... I don't know, like you're missing something important?"

My heart contracted painfully. I *was* missing something important. Four pieces of my soul, to be exact. Four sets of eyes that had wormed their way into my heart. Four men who were as different as the four seasons, but who had each become an integral part of my life. Hell, I even missed Akio.

You can go back to them, I told myself, trying to ease the ache in my chest. *As soon as you remove the tracking spell, you can go back.*

A mean little voice in the back of my head reminded me that's exactly what I'd thought when I left Wyoming. But even after Edgar died and I was free to go wherever I wanted, I hadn't been able to work up the courage to go back and look for Corin. It had been too long by then; I'd changed too much. And like a coward, I'd been too afraid to face the consequences of my actions.

Fighting a rising wave of self-disgust, I pressed up from my slouch. "I'm okay, Ivy. Thanks for worrying though, it's sweet of you. I'm going to go change."

I stood slowly and trudged to my room, my limbs feeling like lead. My mood brightened briefly as I sorted through my meager wardrobe, picking out a pair of soft dark-wash jeans and a black tank top. But as soon as I was dressed like myself again, darkness settled back over me like a storm cloud. I sank down on the bed, rubbing a hand absently over my heart, as if I could massage away the pain.

Was this awful feeling an effect of the bond straining as I was separated from my four? Or was it simply because I missed them? It was becoming harder and harder to separate my feelings for the men from the magical bond that connected me to them.

Did it even really matter? Regardless of the reason, I had

become attached to them in a way I'd never expected, and there was no way to talk my body, mind, and soul out of yearning for them.

Sadness and exhaustion hit me like a right hook, and I curled up on the bed, pulling a pillow over my head.

I'd give myself an hour to wallow in self-pity, but then I was going to hunt down the bastard who put this tracking charm on me and break it—and them.

WHEN I OPENED my eyes again, all I saw was darkness.

I blinked, shoving off the pillow I had buried my head under in my sleep. But the darkness remained.

Shit. What time was it?

There were so few working streetlights left in this neighborhood that only the watery blue light of the moon filtered into my room. It took several moments for my eyes to adjust to the dark, and even then, all I could make out were vague shadows. Something had woken me. But what?

I strained my ears, trying to pick up any unusual sounds. The TV still droned on, filling the apartment with ambient noise, but that was all I could hear.

Sliding off the bed, I padded to the living room in bare feet. The lights were off in here too, and Ivy's ghostly form was pale in the TV's flickering glow.

"Ivy?" I whispered.

"Hmm?" Her gaze was locked on the TV, where a middle-aged woman showed off a set of glittering bangle bracelets made of magic stones that apparently made the skin of her hands smoother. Another woman exclaimed over the jewelry's beauty and value, reminding the audience that the set was available now for a low, low price.

"Ivy!" I hissed again.

"Hmm?"

"Did you hear anything just now?"

She muttered something that sounded like a "no," although I wasn't sure that meant much. If it wasn't coming out of the TV, I doubted she'd notice a five-piece band marching through here.

"Forget it." I stood stock-still, one hand braced on the back of the couch.

Then I heard it.

Soft footsteps outside.

Low voices.

Shit. Had whoever was tracking me found me already? I'd made it easier for them by going someplace unprotected by any concealment spells.

Then again, they'd made my job easier too, saving me the trouble of hunting them down. We could have this fight right here, right now.

I darted back into the bedroom and pulled a dagger from the rickety bedside table. The blade was slightly curved, and it was longer than my other daggers. Flipping it in my grip, I crept back into the living room, glad for the sound cover the TV provided. The two women were still gushing over the same damn bracelets, their artificially cheerful voices filtering through my apartment.

Ivy didn't even look up as I tiptoed to the door. Flattening myself to the wall beside it, I reached slowly for the handle as the footsteps in the hall grew louder.

When they stopped outside, I yanked the door open with a quick jerk and lunged forward, dagger raised.

CHAPTER 19

"LANA, *NO!*"

A pair of strong arms wrapped around my waist, hauling me away from—

Akio?

The incubus's widened eyes narrowed to slits as he scowled at me and the dagger I still held raised in my right hand.

"Why does this all seem so familiar?" he drawled.

"Akio?" I could already tell who was behind me, but I twisted in his arms to look anyway. "Fenris?"

The wolf shifter grinned, releasing his grip. "Hey, killer. You really think we'd let you get away that easily?" He called softly down the hall, "Guys! We found her!"

"I—"

My half-formed thought was interrupted by the sight of Jae and Corin rounding the corner. Corin stormed toward me, his features twisted in rage, his blue eyes blazing.

Unconsciously, I retreated a few steps, slipping back into my apartment. He followed, hitting the door so hard it banged off the wall. He stalked forward, invading my space, looming over me.

"*Again?*" His voice was almost unrecognizable it was so full of anger and pain. "Is this your fucking signature move? Sneaking out when no one's watching like some kind of godsdamned ghost?"

"Hey!" Ivy put her hands on her hips indignantly. She'd turned around on the couch to watch us; apparently, the spectacle of four men bursting into my apartment was better entertainment than a late-night infomercial.

Corin didn't even spare a glance for the ghost. He was breathing heavily, his chest rising and falling like he'd run all the way here, and his eyes were locked on me. The other three men gathered behind him, watching silently.

"Well?" he demanded in a choked voice. "Aren't you going to tell us it was for our own good? That you *had* to leave? That it was all part of some noble plan to save us?"

I straightened my spine, despite the overbearing pressure of his presence so close to me. "It was. I—"

"*You don't get to decide that!*" The muscles in his neck strained as he clenched his fists by his sides. When he spoke again, the volume was lower, but the intensity was just as strong. "You. Don't. Get to decide that. And no matter what you tell yourself about it being for our own good, I promise you, it's not."

"So you'd rather I put you in danger? Just because it hurts to leave?" I snapped.

"I want the choice, Lana! I want to be able to decide to make a sacrifice for you like you're so willing to do for me. I want us to fucking *trust* each other, to face the world and whatever shit it throws at us together!" He gestured to the three shadowed figures behind him. "These men have been my teammates for three years. I would kill for them. I would die for them. And I would *never* leave them behind. They're my *team.* My *family.* They know what that fucking means. Do you?"

I swallowed, my mouth dry. My skin felt too tight, stretched over my muscles and bones like a drum. I stared up at the man who had marched into my darkened apartment like a whirlwind of anger—but suddenly, all I could see was the boy who had woken up one morning to find the love of his life gone without a trace. The panic, the confusion, the soul-crushing *loss* that boy had experienced danced like a horrible echo across Corin's face in the dim light of the TV.

Tears welled and ran down my face, mirroring the ones that slid over Corin's flushed cheeks. The dagger dropped from my hand, but the clatter as it hit the floor barely reached my ears.

He shook his head, brushing a hand over his eyes.

"You broke my heart when you left me and Margie behind, Lana. You broke it again today. Do it one more time, and there'll be nothing left."

"I... I'm sorry, Corin. I'm so sorry," I whispered, my lips trembling.

Grabbing me roughly, Corin pulled me into his arms,

enveloping me in a hug so tight I could barely breathe. I didn't care. Oxygen hardly seemed important right now.

"Don't you understand?" he murmured after a moment, his voice rumbling in my ear as I pressed my cheek to his chest. "When I say we're better off together *no matter what*, I mean it. And I will always mean it. I would rather die by your side than live without you."

His words cracked my heart, but the pain felt good. Like a broken limb being reset so it could heal properly.

"I just don't want you to get hurt." My words were muffled against his chest.

"Then stop fucking running off on me," Corin shot back with a slight chuckle before lifting my chin. "I don't want to see you get hurt either. None of us do. That's why we've gotta stick together, right? So we can protect each other."

I nodded, wiping my cheeks with the back of my hand as I pulled away. I hadn't felt this girly in a long time, but strangely, I wasn't embarrassed about it in the presence of these four.

My ghost roommate still watched us intently, her brown doe eyes wide. The light from the abandoned TV flickered over the faces of the men in front of me, highlighting their features in blues and grays.

I shot a glance at Akio.

"Sorry about the...." I picked up the dagger, gesturing to it limply before setting it on the little table by the door.

He rolled his eyes. "I'm growing used to it."

I guessed his half acceptance of my half apology was about as good as we were going to get. I felt connected to Akio as strongly as to the others, but a wall still existed between us that I wasn't sure how to break through.

"I'm with Corin, killer." Fenris pulled me into his arms, pressing a kiss to the top of my head. His body was firm and warm, and I let my hands skate over the strong muscles of his back before pulling away awkwardly. "Don't ever scare us like that again. I thought I'd go out of my mind when we came back and you were gone. Akio was so worked up he practically yanked all his hair out, and nobody needs a bald incubus."

Akio snorted, but he wouldn't meet my gaze when I looked over at him. Had he really been that worried about me? Something in my chest felt warm and gooey at the thought.

I drew back suddenly, taking in the four of them. "Wait. How the hell did you find me, anyway?"

Jae's lips tilted in his calm smile. "That was Fenris's doing."

"Yup. You told me all about where you live, remember? Including that creepy-as-fuck clown mural on the front of the building. We asked around, and one of the Resistance members used to rent a place around here. He knew what I was talking about as soon as I said 'magic clown' and told us how to get here."

"I drove your car here. We thought you might need it," Jae added, then his face darkened. "That thing is truly...." He shook his head, looking pained.

I knew it. This quiet, contemplative mage was a total car nerd. Then again, someone didn't have to be that into cars to recognize that mine was a wretched specimen.

Ivy cleared her throat loudly, drawing my attention. "Hello! Aren't you going to introduce me?"

"Oh, sorry! Ivy, meet Corin, Jae, Akio, and Fenris. Guys, this is Ivy. She, uh, lives here too."

The ghost beamed and waved at the four men, who hesitantly waved back. Corin shot me a curious glance, and I just shrugged. He grinned.

My heart swelled. Godsdamn it, that was one of the most beautiful sights in the world.

I'd missed his lopsided grin, and the way his clear blue eyes danced with humor, as if the two of us were in on a joke the rest of the world didn't get. I knew it would probably be a while before the mess of emotions between us finally resolved itself, but for now, I vowed to earn his trust back by proving I wouldn't disappear ever again.

"Do you want to watch TV with me?" Ivy asked eagerly. "This is a really good show!"

Deciding not to ask what made one infomercial better than another, I shook my head. "Sorry, Ivy. We've got some important business to discuss."

"Suit yourself."

She turned around and plopped back on the sofa, instantly absorbed again by the bright images flickering on the screen. The rest of us gathered around my beat-up table, Akio leaning against the half wall separating my kitchen and living room while everyone else pulled out chairs. I still wasn't sure what time it was. Late, I knew that, but now that the guys were here, I was suddenly wide-awake.

"I'm..." I cleared my throat. "I can't say I'm sorry you all found me, but the fact remains: as long as I'm carrying this tracking spell, it's not safe for anyone to be near me."

"That's why we need to break the spell," Fenris said, as the rickety chair he settled into creaked ominously. He was carrying too many pounds of sculpted muscle for my shitty-ass furniture to handle.

"Yeah, but how? I have no idea who created it or who put it on me. It could—" I broke off, my brow furrowing. "Godsdamn it. Son of a bitch!"

"What?" Jae leaned forward.

"Rat!"

"Excuse me?"

"Rat. The go-between connecting me and my employers. He was the last person I saw before I went to Akio's house for the job. And when he touched my hand, it felt like a shock went up my arm. I didn't think anything of it then, figured it was just because he was so fucking cold. It must have been him. I can't believe he sold me out! I thought he hated the Gifted as much as I did."

"He very well may, but that makes no difference. Money and power can bend morals—or break them entirely." Jae's green eyes clouded over. It was a look I was beginning to recognize, some remembered pain pulling his attention inward. I slid my hand across the table to cover his, and his expression cleared as he met my eyes. Shaking his head slightly, he continued, "But if you think it was him, that's a good thing. It gives us a place to start in the hunt for the mage who created the tracking spell."

"I know where he usually hangs out," I said, thinking of the seedy bar where I'd first met Rat. He was well under the drinking age, but in that place, a four-year-old could toddle in and order two fingers of whiskey.

"Good." Jae ran a long finger over his chin. "We need to find him quickly. The concealment spell on the Resistance headquarters is strong, so searching for it is as difficult as trying to crack a complex code—unless you have a key. The tracking spell is the key. As long as our enemy has that, they will manage to break the code and see through the concealment spell. We need to destroy the tracker at its source before that happens. I'll put a masking spell on you as well, which should slow them down a bit."

I picked viciously at a chip in the wood veneer of the table. Every time we discussed the tracking spell I carried, my skin crawled. It felt like I was host to some kind of magical parasite. I was half tempted to run across the room, grab my dagger, and try to dig the thing out of my flesh.

But hell, if Rat was the one who had sold me out and stuck me with this fucking spell, I was more than happy to use my blade on him instead. In fact, nothing sounded better at the moment.

"What time is it, anyway?" I asked, glancing around the table.

Corin pulled what must've been a new burner phone from the Resistance out of his pocket, pressing a button on the side. "Just after midnight."

A smile split my face.

Perfect.

CHAPTER 20

THE CROW'S Nest thumped with a loud beat I felt in my bones as much as heard with my ears. During the day, this place looked like any other abandoned building on the block, with one small window at the front so covered in grime you couldn't even see inside. But at night, the flickering green neon sign of a crow and the heavy pulse of music called to the disenfranchised denizens of the Outskirts looking to drink or fuck their troubles away.

I'd come here the first time simply because of the name, and I kept coming back because the drinks were decent and cheap. Mostly cheap.

When we walked in, every head in the place snapped up and then immediately ducked back down again. It wasn't surprising. The five of us must pack a pretty big wallop of power. It was extremely rare for the Gifted to go slumming in the Outskirts, and when they did venture out this far from the city center, it was never for anything good. The general approach most Blighted took if they encountered a magic user outside the Capital was to shut the hell up and look the other way.

Trying not to be hurt that people who had once been my confederates would no longer even look me in the eye, I led the men through the long, narrow room, past the bar running down one side of it to the back, where the space opened up into a larger area with booths, a few tables, and a pool table that never had all its balls.

Scanning the space, I spotted Rat in a dark booth tucked into a corner.

He had his arm wrapped around a thin woman with black hair and big eyes. She clutched her glass tightly and seemed far more enthralled by its contents than by whatever Rat was whispering in her ear. It was obvious even from where I stood that she wasn't interested in the scrawny young man, but she'd probably stick around as long as he was buying.

I tugged on Jae's arm and jerked my head toward the couple, then veered in their direction, my four right behind me. A path cleared for us, and as we approached Rat's table, he glanced up. His eyes bugged out when he caught sight of me, and he scrambled to rise. Before he could escape, I slid into the booth beside him, boxing him in between me and the dark-haired girl on his other side.

"Gee, Rat, are you two-timing me? I really thought we had something." I let the threat hang heavy in my voice.

The girl's terrified eyes met mine for a brief moment before she slipped out of the booth and hustled away through the crowd, leaving her drink behind. I hated that we were taking advantage of the fear the Blighted had of the Gifted, but it was better for everyone that she left. Akio slid in to take her place, Jae beside him. Fenris and Corin stationed themselves in front of the booth, blocking any attempted escape.

"Lana?" Rat stammered. "Oh, hey, doll. What are you—I was just—"

He cleared his throat, grabbed his erstwhile date's abandoned drink, and tossed it back in one gulp. Any doubts I'd had that this skinny little dick was the one who betrayed me were quickly evaporating.

"Thirsty?" I arched an eyebrow.

He laughed, a thin, high-pitched noise. "Well, you know how it is. Just having a few drinks to unwind. We work hard. We deserve a little—"

"What you deserve—" I interrupted, digging the dagger I'd been hiding into the soft flesh between his ribs, pressing just hard enough to let him know I was serious "—is to be gutted like a rabbit for selling me out to the fucking Gifted."

He winced, holding his breath, and I eased off the pressure a little bit so he could draw in air.

"I don't... I don't know what you're talking about, doll."

"Really? Should I see if my friends here can jog your memory? It might not be pleasant, but I'm sure they can help you figure out what you did."

As I spoke, Jae casually turned his hand over, and a small ball of blue flame burst from it, hovering over his palm. Akio's dark eyes glittered in the blue light, mesmerizing as twin galaxies. He could probably charm Rat into telling us everything, but I wanted to exhaust every other option first. Akio's powers still scared the fuck out of me—probably because I feared how easily he could use them on me.

Rat jerked back like he'd been shocked, almost impaling himself on my blade with the sudden move. "Oh fuck! No, no! I remember. I know! You don't have to—"

I poked him with the dagger again, pulling his focus back to me as Jae snuffed the magical flame. "So it *was* you? You put a tracking spell on me?"

He gulped, his big Adam's apple bobbing in his skinny neck.

"Yeah, I did. I'm sorry, doll. I didn't know you were... one of them." His eyes darted nervously around the booth, taking in each of my companions.

"So if you'd known I was Gifted, you wouldn't have fucked me over, but when you thought I was just another Blighted, it was perfectly fine? You know that's fucked up, right? What about solidarity? This is how the Gifted keep us down. They get us to sell each other out as we fight over the little scraps they throw us."

I knew it wasn't technically correct anymore to count myself as part of that "us," but I didn't feel comfortable lumping myself in with the Gifted either.

"Right. Exactly! They—they keep us down." Rat's bulbous nose and gaunt cheeks were red, and a thin veneer of sweat made his forehead glisten in the dim light. He was babbling now, agreeing with whatever I said to try to save his own skin.

"Forget it, Rat. Just tell me what you know about this spell and who made it."

"I—" He broke off, beady eyes darting around the bar nervously.

Keeping the pressed knife firmly against him, I raised my other hand. A flash of orange fire burst from it, and out of the corner of my eye, I saw Jae smile proudly. Rat, on the other hand, shrieked like a pre-pubescent girl and scrambled backward, pressing his gangly body into the back of the booth seat so hard it was like he was hoping the cracked vinyl would absorb him.

I moved my hand closer to his face, letting him feel the heat of the fire dancing above my palm. A feeling of power shot through me, followed quickly by a roiling wave of nausea.

Don't become like them, Lana. Don't let magic corrupt you.

"Okay, okay! I'll tell you." Rat's voice was a high-pitched whisper.

Closing my hand into a fist, I snuffed the flame, satisfaction at my victory dampened by self-disgust. "Good. Then talk."

He ducked his head and spoke so low I had to lean closer to hear him over the music. "I don't know who made the tracking spell. But it came from someone in the government. There's a guy who always meets me in the tunnels under the People's Palace. He gave it to me. It's nothing special!" he added hastily. "They put trackers on a lot of the mercenaries they hire… so they can keep an eye on where they go. He called it a 'precaution.' In case the merc betrays them or leads them to a bigger target."

My skin chilled. Well, fuck. That was exactly what I'd done.

"Where is the receiver kept?" I pressed.

"I don't know. I never—" Rat stopped. "Wait, wait. I had to meet him inside the palace once." His eyes darted back and forth, and he licked his lips. "He came out of a room that had a bunch of maps on the walls. A guard hustled me away right quick, but I got a little peek inside. Something was glowing in the corner."

Trying to contain my excitement, I shot a look at Jae.

The mage nodded thoughtfully, his green eyes considering Rat. "Yes, that could be where the tracking receivers are. But the People's Palace is enormous. You're going to have to give us more than 'a room with maps' for us to find it."

Rat gulped, bobbing his head. "Right. It was, um, in the south wing. On the fifth floor." He looked around the group, trying to gauge whether the information he'd provided was enough. At our stony faces, he continued spewing words. "It was at the end of a hall. With a big door. There were portraits on the walls. The carpet was green!"

Jae tapped his long fingers on the table. "Now, that might help."

My brow furrowed. "Green carpet?"

"Yes. The floors in the grand ballroom and other large spaces are marble, and most of the hallways are carpeted in red. Green narrows it down."

"It was green! Definitely green." Rat's eagerness to please made me feel a little sick. If I'd believed for one second that he was helping us to right the wrong he'd done, I'd be proud of him. But I knew he was just doing it because right now we were a bigger threat to his life than the Gifted official who'd hired him. The worst part was, I couldn't even blame him. I'd spent the past eight years doing pretty much what he was doing now, working as a lackey for the Gifted and convincing myself that my motivations weren't entirely selfish.

Rat's sweaty face shone in the flickering red and blue lights of the bar. Stubble grew in little patches on his chin and jawline. For fuck's sake, the kid couldn't even grow a full beard. He shouldn't be sitting in a seedy bar at one in the morning having covert talks about government tracking spells. I didn't particularly like Rat, but I wanted a better life for him than this.

"That's it?" I asked. "Anything else you can tell us?"

He ran a rand through his damp mop of hair. "Nothing. I swear. I don't know the guy's name. He's older. Tallish, with brown hair."

I pulled my dagger away from his ribs, and his shoulders drooped with relief, making him look like a deflating balloon.

"Thanks, Rat. Take care of yourself, okay? Maybe look into a new line of work?"

"Yeah. Yeah, I will. Thanks, doll."

His confidence seemed to be returning now that he was no longer at knifepoint, and I could take a guess at the thoughts floating through his head. He was probably trying to figure out a way to trade news of my visit for protection from the Gifted government. There was no loyalty among the desperate.

I switched the grip on my knife and angled back toward him, but Akio held up a hand. "I'll take care of this."

He inclined his head, speaking low in Rat's ear as Jae stood up, tugging me out of the booth with him. I couldn't tear my gaze away from Rat's face. His jaw went slack, his eyes fell out of focus, and a look of pure bliss crossed his features. He nodded slowly, agreeing with whatever the incubus murmured.

After a few moments, Akio leaned back and slid out of the booth, leaving the gangly teen staring off into space.

"What did you do?" I stopped myself from waving a hand in front of Rat's face, but I was pretty sure he wouldn't have noticed if I had.

"I told him to forget we were here. He did."

Akio's face was unreadable, but the colored lights of the bar illuminating his chiseled features made him look like a painting of a god. It was probably because he was still giving off echoes of the charm he'd used on Rat, but I had the strongest urge to trace the line of his cheekbone, to caress the soft skin of his lips with my thumb... or *my* lips.

His dark eyes met mine, burning with heat, and I stepped back unconsciously. How did he always manage to put me so off balance? I hated never knowing if the reaction I had to him was genuine, or if he was luring me in with his incubus powers.

"Great. Then let's get the fuck out of here," I muttered, turning away from the booth where a slack-jawed Rat still sat like a statue.

The chill night air hit me as I stepped outside, and I turned my face into the breeze, letting it cool my skin.

"You think his info was good?" Fenris asked Jae behind me as we walked to my car.

"I don't think he was lying. It's as good a place to start as any. We already suspected the Representatives were behind this, and narrowing down the possible location inside the People's Palace helps immensely."

I pulled hard on the finicky handle, wrenching the driver's side door open and looking over the car at the men.

"So all we have to do is break into the People's Palace, sneak into a restricted room, and destroy the receiver? Right. No biggie." I raised my brows at Corin. "You still sure you don't want me to run away?"

He grinned fiercely at me. "Never."

CHAPTER 21

SHARING a room with four men isn't easy.

It's especially difficult if that room is in a cramped, run-down apartment barely big enough for one person, let alone five.

But we managed somehow.

I offered up the couch, ignoring Ivy's horrified look, but none of my four wanted to be that far away from me. Despite my frequent assurances that I wouldn't try to skip out on them again, I think they were all still a little anxious after my vanishing act earlier. And if I was being honest with myself, I wanted them close by too. I was still uncertain exactly how I felt about the bond between us, or how to handle having such strong and conflicting feelings for four different people—but I couldn't deny the bond was there, pulling me toward them at all times.

So I scrounged up extra blankets and stole a few pillows from the couch, and the men all stretched out on the floor near the bed. And despite everything looming over us, I slept better with them in the room than I had in a long time.

When light peeked through the slats in the worn wooden blinds, I blinked my eyes open slowly.

Still early.

I let my lids fall shut again, making a little sound of contentment as I yawned. In the sleepy early morning glow, my defenses were lower, and I let myself revel for a moment in the sound of four people breathing softly around me, the unique scent of each man mingling with the others in the air, and the feel of the large, warm palm resting on my hip.

Wait.

What?

My lids popped open, and I flipped over to my other side, meeting Fenris's chocolate brown eyes.

"Fen!" I whispered indignantly.

He grinned sheepishly at me. "I got cold."

His hand had stayed on me when I turned over, and now it caressed my opposite hip, his touch sparking a fire deep in my belly.

I cocked one eyebrow up. "You got cold? So you decided to sneak under the covers with me? Why didn't you cuddle up with Jae? He has the biggest blanket."

"Well, no offense to Jae," Fenris said, his voice a low rumble, "but I don't think he's as cuddly as you are."

My heart skipped in my chest, panic and pleasure warring in my mind. It would be so easy to give in to the pull of the bond, to follow the tug that felt completely natural and stop struggling against it at every turn. But I'd spent years of my life under a corrupt man's sway, and when Edgar died, I vowed I'd never let anyone else have power over me. This wasn't the same; I knew that—I *felt* that—but it didn't stop my primal instinct to fight against something that felt so out of my control.

I pressed a hand to his chest. Maybe because I wanted to keep some distance between us, or maybe just because I wanted to feel the hard planes of his muscles and the heat of his skin through his T-shirt.

"You don't feel cold to me," I accused.

He smiled, revealing a line of even white teeth. "Well, I'm not anymore." The hand on my hip slipped around to my lower back, tugging me a little closer. I fisted his shirt, my breath coming faster. His stubble was thicker today, and I wondered if it would feel scratchy or smooth against my skin.

Fenris skimmed his hand up the side of my body, over the curve of my shoulder, and rested it on my cheek, running the rough pads of his fingers along my jawbone.

Was he going to kiss me?

Did I want him to?

"Coffee!" I blurted, louder than I intended.

"Hmm?" Jae murmured from somewhere near the foot of the bed. Fenris cocked an eyebrow at me, looking at me with mild amusement.

"I'll just… make some coffee," I muttered, sliding backward out of bed, almost falling off the mattress in my haste to escape. I grabbed my pants off the headboard—I'd removed them last night under the covers—and yanked them on, darting out the door.

Ivy glanced up at me as I banged around the kitchen making more noise than I should have this early in the morning. But nerves jangled through my body. I didn't have the mental capacity to handle all the thoughts vying for attention in my brain right now, and I was pinning my hopes on the belief that coffee would help.

Either Fenris had almost kissed me, or I'd almost kissed him. Either way, what the hell did that mean? When Asprix had informed us we were all connected by my magic, I hadn't known how blurry the line was going to get between the magical bond and a physical, emotional, and mental one.

I wasn't used to any of this. After I left Wyoming, I'd been such a mess emotionally that I hadn't even thought about a relationship for years. I had made a half-hearted and disastrous attempt at a one-night stand a couple years ago, but the truth was, I'd been determinedly and happily a loner.

Until Corin came back into my life.

Until Fenris, Jae, and Akio cracked open my heart and made room for themselves in there too.

Perching on a wobbly chair, I watched the coffee pot until it stopped brewing, then leapt up to pour a cup, gulping down the scalding liquid too fast.

"H-hot!"

I was breathing through my mouth with my tongue hanging out like a dog when Corin wandered into the room, followed closely by Jae and Fenris. The wolf shifter was tugging on his pants, and I felt a flush heat my cheeks.

Snapping my jaw shut, I looked down at my steaming coffee. "Where's Akio?"

"Primping." Fenris smirked, nudging me out of the way to reach for the coffee. My small kitchen was feeling tinier by the second.

Corin slipped his phone into his pocket, leaning on the half wall between the kitchen and living room. "I updated Christine. She's on board with us breaking into the palace to destroy the tracking spell's receiver. Another couple of houses got hit last night—closer to the Resistance's location."

Fenris swore softly, rifling through my cabinets in search of a mug. "Damn. Then we don't have much time."

It was my turn to move him out of the way, pushing him aside so I could pull a mug out of the cabinet by the fridge. It was my backup mug, glazed blue with a huge yellow moon on it. It seemed appropriate for Fen.

"We don't," Corin agreed. "Anybody got any brilliant ideas how to get inside the palace?"

"Can we use a transport spell?" I asked, handing the mug to Fen.

He took it with a grin. "Nah. There are protections on the palace that keep people from being able to transport in. You might be able to use one to get out, but definitely not in."

"Well, shit. That was my one brilliant idea."

"The Grand Ball is being held at the People's Palace in two days," Jae offered.

I chugged the rest of my still-hot coffee, then rinsed the mug and set it on the counter. It and the blue one were the only mugs I had, and I felt bad hogging it. "So how does the Grand Ball help us?"

"Because I have an invitation." Jae spoke simply, but a

slight blush crept into his cheeks when I rounded on him, eyes wide.

"You *what?*"

"My whole family does. My father is the Minister of Justice, so he's invited to a lot of events in the Capital."

I blinked.

Jae was so unlike any other Gifted person I'd met that I sometimes forgot he was one of them. But the truth was, the world of wealth, privilege, and power he came from was the complete opposite of the world I'd lived in all my life.

I blinked again.

The mage's elegant features flushed a deeper red, and he looked away, staring down at the table and tapping absently at the faded wood veneer. Was his hand shaking?

"That's perfect!" Fenris exclaimed. "We'll need to get Lana in too, and maybe Corin can sneak in with the Blighted staff."

"I'm allowed a plus-one," Jae said stiffly. "Lana can be my date."

I had a million questions for him, but he looked so abjectly miserable that I shoved them all down. He didn't need me poking and prodding him, bringing more attention to the privileged upbringing he'd had, and whatever it was about that upbringing that caused him so much pain.

"Date? For what?" Akio drawled, walking out of the bedroom.

His dark jeans were slung low on his hips, and he wasn't wearing a shirt. Considering he'd had more time than any of us to get dressed, that could only be intentional. I wanted to roll my eyes at his vanity—but they were too busy trying to take in the intricate tattoos that covered both of his arms like sleeves, winding over and around his shoulders to meet on his chest. When he walked over to the counter to grab my now-empty mug, I almost gasped. The tattoos continued on his back, his muscles rippling under a black ink design so detailed I could spend hours studying it.

Holy gods. Fucking beautiful.

Someone else had answered his question, and when I shook off the fog of lust clouding my brain and rejoined the conversation, they were discussing the best way for me to find the green carpeted hallway in the palace.

"It shouldn't be too difficult for her to slip away for a few minutes," Jae said. "The ball will be well attended, so one guest missing for a few minutes will be easily overlooked. But actually getting into any restricted areas will be harder. The palace is always heavily guarded, and security will be ramped up for the event."

"Well, we already know she's good at illusion spells." Akio leaned against my kitchen counter, regarding me coolly.

"True. But all the palace guards wear charms that allow them to see through illusions. What she needs more than that is the power of suggestion."

My gaze flicked between the two of them. "The what?"

"Charm," Akio clarified.

"Oh." I blanched. "Like... what you do?"

"Of course." He arched a brow. "Like what you do too, kitten. If Asprix is right, you should be able to charm someone as well as any succubus."

Kitten?

I ground my teeth. There was a knife in the kitchen drawer right next to him. One more little stab wound wouldn't kill him, right?

"You know, I prefer Fen's nickname for me," I told him pointedly, but all I got in return was a devilish smile.

"I'm sure you do, kitten. I just don't love the memories it brings up, so I thought I'd put my own spin on it."

Turning my back on him, I raised a brow at Jae. *"This* is the guy who's going to teach me how to be charming?"

Half a breath later, I felt a warm body behind me, and a pair of lips brushed the shell of my ear. I froze, surprised by the sudden movement.

"I assure you, Lana, I can be very charming when I choose to be," Akio's velvety voice whispered softly—so softly it was as if the words slipped into my brain without actually being spoken. My name on his lips sent a sharp zing of pleasure straight down to my core, and my knees actually buckled.

I stumbled forward, catching myself before I went down like a puppet with its strings cut. Cheeks flaming, I turned around and shoved the demon's perfect tattooed chest, hard.

"Don't *ever* do that! Do not use your godsdamned incubus charm on me. You think that's fucking funny?"

Akio stepped back, holding up his hands. His face was as carefully neutral as always, but for a moment something like hurt flashed in his eyes. I clenched my jaw. *Yeah, right.* Maybe he was just disappointed he hadn't been able to make me do any party tricks, like hop on one foot or bark like a dog.

The kitchen fell into an awkward silence, broken only by the sound of cartoons floating in from the living room.

After a few moments, Fenris cleared his throat.

"So… can you teach her?" he asked, his voice artificially light.

Akio's dark gaze caught mine. "Yes."

"Great! And… you'll learn, right?" Fen's brows scrunched together as he turned to me, and I chuckled at his concern, pressing my finger between his eyes to smooth the wrinkle.

"Yeah. I mean, I'll try."

"Perfect!" Fenris beamed, grabbing my hand and kissing the back of it. "Then turn on the charm, killer."

CHAPTER 22

As it turned out, charm wasn't a quality or a skill that came naturally to me.

Despite my promise to Fen, the lesson with Akio did not go well. I'd never needed to be charming in my life, so my learning curve was incredibly steep. And having a cranky-as-fuck incubus drill instructor hovering over my shoulder nitpicking every move I made didn't help much either.

It took most of the morning before I even got close to performing an actual demon charm, and all my failures leading up to that point were epic. There was a lot of fake eyelash batting, hip swaying, and over-the-top lip licking. Even Fenris, who normally gazed at me like he wanted to devour me no matter what I did, winced awkwardly as I tilted my head coyly in front of him, pursing my lips into what was supposed to be an alluring pout.

I mean, fuck. If I couldn't even get Fen to bite, then how

the hell was I supposed to charm a complete stranger? And a palace guard, no less?

Finally, Akio pulled me aside and gave me a stern lecture about how true charm didn't come from external tricks and gimmicks, but from inner power and confidence. I wanted to ask him why he spent so much time fixing his hair every morning if that was true, but bit down on my tongue so hard I tasted blood instead.

The incubus's pointers actually helped though, and by midafternoon, I was able to get both Fenris and Corin into a suggestible state. I couldn't practice on Jae because he'd headed back to the Capital; he needed to put in an appearance in his old life and make arrangements for us to attend the Grand Ball. And I refused to poke my finger into the morass of antagonism and attraction that pulsed between me and Akio, which left the human and shifter as my only guinea pigs.

The next day, while Fen and Corin worked out more details of our plan, Akio took me outside to practice on a new test subject. I wasn't keen on the idea, but he insisted I needed to charm at least one total stranger before he'd consider me ready for our mission.

"What about that guy?"

I jerked my chin toward a man walking down the street toward us. He was short and stocky, with a wide nose and shaggy brown hair that brushed his shoulders. He gave off a nervous energy, and as soon as he got close enough to feel our magic, he veered away, darting across the street.

Akio folded his arms, leaning against the side of a weathered brick building. "He'll work. If you can catch him."

Shit. I sprang into action, following the man. He shot a look over his shoulder, peering at me through the curtain of his hair, then picked up his pace.

"Sir! Wait! I don't mean you any harm. I just want to ask you a question."

I caught up to him and put a hand on his shoulder. His body tensed, but before he could make a run for it, I leaned toward him, pouring every bit of charm I could muster up into his ear like honey.

"Relax. Just stay here with me. Don't think about anything but my voice. Forget the rest of the world; just let me in."

He softened slightly, and I ran my fingertips along the muscles of his shoulder, charming him through physical touch as well. I continued to speak low in his ear, whispering literal sweet nothings. According to Akio, it was less important *what* I said than how I said it. When I got good enough, I should be able to charm someone by repeating "broccoli" over and over —or not speaking at all.

After a moment, I stepped in front of the man to peer at his face. He had that loopy, blissed out look that churned my stomach. Gods, this creeped me out. But at least I'd proven I could do it. I looked to Akio for confirmation, and he pushed languidly off the wall to join us, crossing the street to circle around me and the hapless Blighted man.

"You should have been able to do this from the other side of the street," Akio pointed out. "The intimacy of proximity helps, but you shouldn't rely on it. The more distractions there are, the more difficult it is to charm someone. That's why it's not a frequently used fight tactic."

I tilted my head. "But you charmed that witch back at your house."

"I was desperate. I needed to stop her from getting her hands on you. And I was only able to put her in a mildly suggestible state at first. But it was enough to give me a chance to get close and fully charm her." He smiled wickedly at me. "And I'm very good."

Choosing to ignore that, I turned back to the charmed man in front of me. "Can I let him go now?"

"First, test your work."

I grimaced, but leaned toward the man, and murmured, "Rub your belly."

He lifted one hand and made slow circles over his belly, like someone who was very drunk and very hungry. Akio nodded approvingly, and I whispered again, "Okay, stop. Go back to whatever you were doing. And forget all about this."

The man blinked, his thick eyebrows furrowing. His eyes still a bit glazed, he turned away from us and walked haltingly down the street.

"You're ready," Akio said, and despite my misgivings, my chest swelled a bit with pride—until he spoke again. "As you'll ever be."

Ah, there's that famous incubus charm.

THE WOMAN in front of me was almost unrecognizable. Her red hair was piled on her head in an elaborate up-do of curls and pins. Her eyes were lined with black, their light gray hue accentuated by the shadow brushed over her lids. Her lips glistened ruby-red.

But it was her dress that truly completed the picture. It was a full-length, dark teal evening gown with embellished floral appliqués across the fitted strapless bodice. A few of the appliqués trailed down the full skirt, making it look like beautiful vines twined around her body.

Is that woman really me?

The full-length mirror in my room was cracked and smudged, but even those defects couldn't hide the stunning beauty of the woman standing before it. I reached out to trace a finger over the surface of the glass, almost surprised when my reflection moved with me. I'd been half convinced she really was a different person.

Jae had returned from the Capital several hours ago, driving another fancy car—how many of those did he have?— and bearing gifts for all of us. He brought me this stunning dress and gave Corin a tuxedo that should match the uniforms of all Blighted staff at the event. He'd also brought communication charms we could use to maintain contact during our operation. They were more subtle than phones and better for undercover ops.

I blew out a breath, puffing my cheeks out. I sure hoped that lady in the mirror felt confident about all of this, because I sure didn't. But we were out of time. Christine had called again this morning to tell Corin that Peacekeepers had been spotted just outside the old factory building that housed the Resistance. The Peacekeepers hadn't been able to see the building through the concealment spell, but they were right on top of it. In very short order, they'd break through the concealment and realize where they were. If we didn't destroy the tracking spell soon, the Resistance would be exposed.

As a precaution, the most vulnerable inhabitants of the headquarters were being moved to alternate locations, but there were risks involved in that as well. Too much movement around the portals would draw unwanted attention to them. The Grand Ball was tonight, and I prayed we wouldn't be too late to prevent the total exposure of the Resistance's location.

You can do this. Lana Crow, badass mercenary, will not be brought down by a palace ball.

I took one last look at myself in the mirror. The only parts of this whole ensemble that made me feel like myself were my necklace, which I refused to take off, and the set of twin daggers strapped to my thighs. Those were another gift from Jae and were hands-down my favorite thing he'd brought back from the Capital.

Resisting the urge to fiddle with my hair any more—Ivy had coached me through both the hair and makeup application, and I wasn't sure how sturdy the up-do actually was—I turned and exited the room.

Fen and Jae had their heads together, setting up the communication charms. Jae was dressed in a perfectly tailored dark gray suit that highlighted the lean lines of his body. Akio fussed over Corin's tuxedo, smoothing out the lines of the jacket while Corin rolled his eyes.

They all looked up when I entered, and the room went quiet.

"What?" I shifted uncomfortably. "Does it not look okay?"

"It looks..." Corin cleared his throat, his nostrils flaring. "You look amazing, Lana."

I scrunched up my face. "Really? I mean, it's not the most practical outfit for a job. At least the skirt is full enough that I can move in it. And it hides my weapons."

Hiking up my skirt, I stretched my legs to make sure I could run without restriction and double-checked that I could reach my blades easily. A choked sound caught my attention, and I glanced up to see all the men staring at my exposed legs.

I flushed, dropping the skirt. "Well, I won't do that during the ball, obviously."

Fen laughed. "Good. I already don't like the Gifted, but if you give them a show like that, I'll hate them all. You're ours, killer. And you're stunning."

The others looked about as uncomfortable with the pronouncement of "ours" as I was. I'd come to truly care for all of them, and I knew with certainty they'd be a part of my life forever. But I still wasn't quite sure what that meant, and Fenris seemed bound and determined to call out this bond between us at every turn.

Noticing the awkwardness that prickled through the room, Fen shot a look around, shrugging. "What? She is."

My face heated, and I scoffed to cover my embarrassment. "Ugh. Shifters! You think all you have to do is slap a sticker that says 'mine' on a woman, and her panties will magically melt off her body."

Twisting a fallen lock of hair between my fingers, I turned to escape back into the bedroom to re-pin it.

But as soon I crossed the threshold, firm hands closed

around my shoulders, spinning me around. Fenris shut the door behind us in a flash and pressed me up against it, his large, warm body boxing me in. His usually laughing brown eyes sparked with a mixture of heat and intensity.

"First of all," he said, his voice low, "I can melt a pair of panties just fine without any stickers, all right? And second of all, I've never told a woman she was mine before. Because no woman ever was... until you."

I sucked in a deep breath, my heart thudding at both his words and the look in his eyes. Shit. He was done joking around about this. My legs wobbled, and I leaned back against the door for stability. Fen's hands were on my upper arms, his body angling toward mine.

"But, fine. If you're not ready to hear that, I can wait. Someday, you will be. In the meantime, know this." He slid one large hand down my arm to grasp my smaller one. I had half a mind to pull it back so he wouldn't realize I was trembling, but it was probably way too late for that.

Fen pressed my hand to his chest, where the rapid beat of his heart slammed against my palm. His eyes were full of nothing but truth as he said one word.

"Yours."

The declaration hovered in the air between us, stealing my breath.

Then, like a dam breaking, I fisted his shirt and pulled him toward me, meeting his hungry lips with my own. His mouth crashed into mine, teeth and tongues colliding in a mad dance. Our joined hands were still sandwiched between us, trapped there by the force of our bodies pressing together, trying to get impossibly closer. Fen's other hand roamed over my skin restlessly, as if hoping to memorize every inch of me he could reach.

Fire ignited in my belly, and I wrapped my hand around the back of his neck, exploring his mouth with my tongue. The sharp, clean scent of pine enveloped me, and the overload of sensations pulled a moan from my throat.

Fen made an answering noise in his chest, the sound rough and deep, as if it came from the most primal part of him. Desperate for more, I managed to work our trapped hands free and wrap my arms around him, relishing the feel of his muscles contracting under my touch. I could barely breathe, but I didn't want to pull my mouth from his long enough to fill my lungs. My fingers skimmed up his neck into the back of his hair, running through the soft, thick strands as I deepened our kiss. I gave a little tug on his hair, and his answering growl sent a shiver of promise through me.

Finally, Fen broke away, leaving us both gasping. He pressed his hands to the door on either side of my head and rested his forehead against mine, his body still leaning into me.

I closed my eyes, enjoying the feel of our heavy breaths mingling in the small space between us. My entire body buzzed like a live wire at the same time an incredible feeling of relief spread through me. It was as if a piece of me I didn't even know was missing had suddenly been reclaimed.

As our breathing returned to normal, Fen drew back, his chocolate eyes warm.

"Good gods, killer. I've been wanting to do that since... well, pretty much since I first met you."

I chuckled, smoothing his mussed hair. "I can relate."

Why the hell did I fight this for so long?

Fen's happy smile was one of the most beautiful things I'd ever seen.

Then his brow furrowed, and his gaze shifted up to my hair. I could feel several new escaped tendrils snaking down the nape of my neck.

"Uh, you might need a few more pins."

CHAPTER 23

THE DRIVE to the Grand Ball was quiet. Jae and I took his car, and the other three followed in mine. As soon as we arrived at the People's Palace, Jae and I would have to keep up appearances as two of the wealthy Gifted elite. I hated splitting our team up, but it made the most tactical sense.

Corin would slip into the palace posing as one of the staff, aided by a Resistance member who worked in the kitchens. Akio and Fenris would wait near the palace grounds, staying in contact via communication charms. If all went well, we wouldn't need their help, but they insisted on coming as backup. They'd also be the ones to alert Christine if—*when*—our mission was successful, so she'd know the Resistance was safe. I knew she was preparing for the worst-case scenario, readying her soldiers for battle and evacuating others as quickly as possible, and even though that vote of no confidence hurt my ego a little, I couldn't blame her. She needed to protect her people first and foremost, and even I wasn't fully certain this plan would work.

As we passed through the gate into the Capital, I tried to focus, running through our plan in my head. But the deep brown of Fenris's eyes kept intruding on my thoughts. The sounds he made. The way his hands felt on my body.

I reached up unconsciously, brushing a finger over my lips. Jae glanced over at me. "Are you all right?"

"Huh? Oh, yeah." I shifted in my seat.

"We can do this, Lana. You can do this."

"I know."

Smoothing my skirt for the hundredth time, I shot a glance at Jae. He looked as calm and composed as ever. I was certain everyone in the apartment knew what had happened between me and Fen, but when we'd emerged from the bedroom, slightly flushed and disheveled, no one had commented on it.

Thank the gods.

I wasn't sorry about what I'd done with Fen, but I was still a bit of an emotional mess. There wasn't time to sort all of that out now, though. We had a job to do.

"Can I ask you something?" Jae asked suddenly, and butterflies took off in my stomach.

Oh fuck. How did I explain to him that the way I felt about Fen was a mirror image of the way I felt about all of them? The connection was different with each of them, but the pull was just as strong.

I cleared my throat. "Um, sure."

"When we came to your apartment the other night, and you attacked Akio, why did you use a dagger instead of magic?"

I blinked. That was not the question I'd been expecting. "Oh. I don't know. Habit, I guess. I didn't even think about it."

He took a right turn, and the palace loomed ahead of us. "I thought that might be the case. I noticed you threatened Rat with a blade first before switching to magic at the bar too. It's part of why I've been taking your magical training slow. You need to adjust to having a new kind of weapon at your disposal and start using it instinctually in fights. A danger when you're first learning a new skill is that it can cause paralysis in high-pressure situations. If you have too many options, you'll spend a half second too long trying to decide which one to use, and that half second can be the difference between winning and losing. That's why I brought you those daggers. I want you to have the option of using the weapon you're most comfortable with if you need to defend yourself."

I turned to face him, deeply touched. In profile, his long nose and fine features looked almost ethereal. "Thank you, Jae."

The corner of his lip lifted. "You're welcome. They're enchanted to return to you, by the way, so you won't lose them if you throw them. They'll just materialize a few moments later back in their sheaths."

My jaw dropped open. "Holy fuck! That's amazing!"

Jae's smile widened, and he shifted his eyes from the road to glance at my beaming face. "I thought you might like that."

"I love it!" I brushed a hand over his knee. "Thank you. For everything. Including this dress, though I feel like a bit of a fraud wearing it."

"You're not a fraud, Lana. Plenty of people at the ball tonight will be dripping with gold and diamonds, but all they're doing is covering up the ugliness in their hearts. You're beautiful, inside and out."

For some reason, his words made tears sting my eyes. Maybe it was the way he spoke so simply and calmly, as if completely certain his pronouncement was true.

"Thank you, Jae," I whispered again.

He reached over the center console and took my hand, lacing our fingers together. I squeezed his back, and we stayed that way until we reached the People's Palace.

I'd always thought its name sounded like a bad joke. Nothing about this palace was for "the people." It had been built a few years after the Great Death, when Denver became the new capital of the country. The Gifted government officials who survived had stepped forward to take control in the aftermath of the plague, which seemed like a good thing at first. They'd managed to rein in the most brutal acts of violence against the Blighted and bring some order to the chaos. I hardly remembered those years, but the old-timers at the Blighted settlement had talked bitterly about how they'd trusted the Representatives at first—until it became clear they were only interested in improving life for their own kind.

Twelve stories high at its tallest point and massively wide, the white marble palace loomed on a slight rise over the whole city, even more imposing than the mountains in the distance. The sprawling north and south wings were four stories high at the ends, with staggered levels building up toward the middle like a huge, elaborate layer cake. There was a massive curated lawn with an enchanted fountain in the front, and two angled roads led up to the entrance. I'd seen the palace from a distance plenty of times—it was impossible to spend time in the Capital and *not* see it—but I'd never been this close.

When we pulled up to the front, a blue-haired fairy greeted us, meeting Jae as he stepped smoothly from the car and accepting the mage's keys. I was about to open my door and step out, but Jae reached it first, holding it open and offering me his hand.

Oh, right. Manners. Act like you have some, Lana.

I felt less ridiculous about accepting help climbing out of a car—I was a grown-ass fucking woman, wasn't I?—when I realized it was actually a lot more difficult in a full-length, billowy evening gown. As I negotiated the yards of fabric wrapped around my body and the godsdamned heels I had to wear, I was grateful for Jae's steadying grip.

He tucked my hand into the crook of his elbow and escorted me up the red-carpeted stairs to the palace entrance. Nerves twisted my stomach, more intense than they'd ever been on a job before. The stakes were higher tonight, and I was much further out of my element.

Palace staff ushered us up a set of wide stairs and into a grand ballroom. I tried not to gape, but it was difficult. The entire palace was made of white marble, with gold accents on the molding. The soaring ceilings were even more ornately decorated, and chandeliers made of hundreds of threads of magical light hung from them, casting a warm glow over the people gathered in the ballroom.

Everyone was dressed in decadent evening wear like us, though some of the ladies were weighed down by considerably more jewelry than I wore. All I had on besides my necklace were simple teardrop earrings, one of which was enchanted with a communication charm. I pressed the dangling gem to activate it as we made our way through the crowd.

"Akio? Fenris?"

"Here." Fenris's voice sounded in my ear. "You guys inside?"

"Yes," I murmured.

"Good. Go get 'em, killer."

"And be safe," Akio added.

"We will." I started to nod before catching myself. They were over a mile away, hidden outside the perimeter of the palace grounds.

I left the charm activated so they could hear what was going on and accepted the delicate crystal flute Jae handed me. Champagne popped and fizzed inside it, and I forced myself to take a dainty sip instead of tossing it back in one gulp. I hated the taste of champagne, but I could use a drink to steady my nerves.

Jae and I continued to work our way around the perimeter

of the gigantic space. Every so often, someone would stop him to say hello. He'd introduce me, I'd promptly forget the person's name, they'd kiss my hand, and then we'd move on. I couldn't see the point of these encounters, but apparently they were the main appeal of events like this. Schmoozing.

Well, maybe not for everyone, I corrected myself, as we passed by a couple standing apart from the others, talking to each other in low voices and shooting furtive glances at the crowd around them. Everyone who passed by seemed to give them a wide berth, and I wondered why until I felt the magic radiating from them.

My eyebrows shot up. "Are those—?"

"Blighted?" Jae dipped his head in a subtle nod, steering me away from the couple. "Yes. Though a better name for them would be 'enhanced.' They're Blighted people who are rich enough and connected enough to essentially buy their way into Gifted society. They've likely had magical blood transfusions, undergone multiple DNA altering spells, and are decked out in a vast array of charmed objects and accessories."

I craned my neck to look at them again, trying not to gawk. "Well, it doesn't look like anybody here is falling for it. No one will even talk to them."

"No. They're looked down upon by most Gifted. You can feel their magic, can't you? It's like a patchwork."

"So they betray their own kind to join the Gifted, and the Gifted don't even want them?" I grimaced. "That's all kinds of fucked up."

Jae's hand tightened on my arm. "Power corrupts, Lana.

Some people will do anything to have more of it, no matter what they have to give up."

He was right. It was why the Gifted, despite having so many luxuries and advantages, were constantly plotting and scheming against each other, like they were all racing to the top of a mountain and there could only be one winner.

"Do you see Corin?" I asked, shaking off my dark thoughts and finally allowing myself to drain the last of my champagne.

"There." Jae inclined his head slightly to the left, and I followed the gesture with my gaze. Corin walked through a cluster of middle-aged Gifted women in elegant dresses, collecting empty glasses on a tray.

As he passed by, one of the women ran her manicured hand over his shoulder, down his back, to his ass.

She squeezed, and my vision filled with red.

I clutched Jae's arm hard, making him flinch. The desire to curl my hand into a fist was so strong I was afraid I'd shatter the empty glass I held. I was so furious I could hardly breathe, and it wasn't just because of the possessiveness that flared at the idea of anyone but me touching Corin. It was the casual way she groped him, as if he was less than a person, a *thing* she could treat any way she liked.

Blinking rapidly against the tears of rage that threatened, I clenched my jaw, trying to take in deep breaths through my nose. Corin's gaze lit on us, and he made his way over, accepting a few more empty glasses as he passed through the crowd. When he reached us, Jae pried the glass from my fingers and placed it on his tray.

"Are you okay? What's wrong?" Corin's brow furrowed as he took in my expression.

"That *woman*," I ground out. "She—she just…. Why do they treat you like—"

Corin's face fell, disgust twisting his features. "I know, Lana. I know. But it doesn't matter right now. We have to focus on one thing at a time. You need to break the tracking spell."

Wrestling my emotions under control, I nodded, blowing out a breath.

"Right. Right. Have you gotten the lay of the land at all?"

"Yeah. I've gotta move on in a second," Corin added in a low voice. "But there's a small door on the other side of the room that the staff are coming through. If you can slip out through there, none of the Blighted you run into should give you any trouble. They wouldn't dare interfere with a Gifted guest. From there, you should be able to get to the south wing."

Shooting a glance across the room, I caught sight of the door he was talking about. "Thanks, Corin."

Jae finished his drink and set the empty flute alongside mine on Corin's tray, and then Corin moved away from us through the crowd.

I took a deep breath. "All right, let's get this show on the road."

We altered our course slightly, cutting across the center of the room toward the door on the other side. Although this was clearly a ballroom, no one was dancing yet. Maybe that came later.

Or maybe the Gifted were too fucking stuck up to dance.

We were halfway across the room when a man stepped in front of us. He was tall, with gray-brown hair, piercing green eyes, and a neatly trimmed goatee and mustache. His face looked familiar, and I was trying to figure out where I'd seen him before, when he clapped a hand on Jae's shoulder.

"Jae, my boy. Won't you introduce me to your lovely date?"

CHAPTER 24

My eyes widened.

This man was Jae's father.

No wonder he looked so familiar. I'd spent hours gazing into green eyes that were an almost exact copy of his during my lessons with Jae, although Jae's eyes had a kindness and depth to them I couldn't find in his father's. The man in front of us might as well have been made of ice for all the warmth he radiated.

"Of course," Jae said in a stilted voice I almost didn't recognize. "Lana, this my father, Jonas Nocturne, the Minister of Justice. Sir, this is Lana Crow."

I had to greet the man formally—I knew that—but every fiber of my being rebelled at the idea of voluntarily giving the Minister of Justice my hand. I tried not to flinch when he caught it and raised it to his lips. I could practically feel the cold steel of handcuffs around my wrists already and yanked my hand back a little quicker than was probably polite.

"It's lovely to meet you, Ms. Crow." Jonas's assessing gaze swept over me as he spoke. "Your beauty and power stand out in this crowd like a diamond in a sea of rocks. I must admit, I was surprised to see someone like you on the arm of my son."

Jae went stiff as a board beside me, and I blinked.

What the fuck?

"I consider myself the luckiest woman here, Mr. Nocturne," I shot back, tightening my grip on Jae's arm.

Jonas gave a deep chuckle that didn't reach his eyes. "That's kind of you to say. But if the two of you are drawing jealous eyes, I assure you, you are the cause. Not my son."

I couldn't understand what was happening here. Why was Jonas openly insulting his own son? And why was Jae, who was normally temperate and steady as the North Star, vibrating with tension? I squeezed his arm tighter, trying to give him some of my strength. Beyond that, I wasn't sure what to do. I obviously couldn't start a fistfight or shouting match with his father, however much I might want to.

So instead, I turned to Jae, channeling my best impression of a high society lady. "Darling, I'm simply parched. Let's go get another drink."

He turned to me, staring blankly. I wasn't sure he'd even heard me, but he jerked his head in a nod.

"Lovely to meet you, Ms. Crow," Jonas said, as I pulled Jae away. "Come find me later. I know almost everyone here, and I'm happy to make introductions. I'll make sure you meet the right people."

"Uh, thanks," I called over my shoulder, not missing the fact that he hadn't included Jae in that invitation.

The weight of Jonas's gaze burned into my back as we walked quickly across the dance floor. We'd reached the other side of the large room before Jae finally relaxed somewhat. He released a shuddering breath, and I could sense his internal struggle as he fought to bring himself back under control.

"Are you all right?" I whispered. I had so many more questions than that, but now wasn't the time to poke at his family issues. Jae seemed on the verge of breaking as it was.

"Yes." He nodded, his voice sounding a bit more normal. "I'm sorry about that."

I blinked. "*You're* sorry? I'm sorry! Your dad's an asshole."

Jae released a small puff of air that was probably meant to be a laugh. "Our relationship is… complicated."

"I don't know. He's an asshole; you're not. Seems pretty simple to me."

My anger was growing as I studied Jae. He seemed almost boyish in his pain, like his father's callous words had reduced him to nothing more than a child. But my statement seemed to bolster him a bit, and he made another attempt at a smile, lifting one corner of his mouth.

"My father did make a good point though," Jae said, glancing around us as we hovered near the door Corin had pointed out. "You are both beautiful and powerful, and that combination makes you stand out like blood in the water in this room of sharks. You'll need to be very careful that no one notices you slip out, and return as fast as you can. People will notice your absence if you're gone too long."

Grimacing at his shark analogy, I scanned the room. Jonas had disappeared back into the crowd, and I couldn't see him anywhere. Corin was wending his way through the room near where we'd come in, and I caught his eye immediately.

Subtly, I made our old gesture for *distraction*. He nodded, then changed course suddenly, plowing into another Blighted waiter. The man's tray flew out of his hands, and the fine crystal flutes filled with pale yellow champagne were briefly airborne, glittering in the light of the chandeliers before they crashed to the ground with a tinkling sound.

The women standing nearby screamed as if the entire place was under attack, sweeping their long skirts away from the splashing liquid, and the Blighted man scrambled to clean up the mess.

Without hesitating, I darted through the door into the staff hallway, striding purposefully down the narrow corridor. I encountered one person—a middle-aged man in a tuxedo like Corin's—but as soon as he saw me, he flattened himself so hard to the wall it was like he was trying to become one with the marble. He didn't say a word as I swept past him. As soon as he scurried away, I ducked into a small alcove and closed my eyes, summoning the illusion spell to make myself invisible. The palace guards could still see me with the help of the charms they wore, but no other staff or wayward party guests would be able to.

My sense of direction was good enough that I knew this hall led west, deeper into the bowels of the palace. I turned left at the first opportunity I got, figuring I'd work my way south until I found a staircase. The ballroom was on the second floor, so the green hallway I wanted should be three floors up.

I made it down another long hallway and up a set of stairs before a voice halted me.

"Excuse me, miss! You can't be back here."

Whirling around, I caught sight of a tall man striding toward me. He was dressed in the dark blue and white uniform of a palace guard, with slicked-back black hair and sharp features.

"Oh!" I put a hand to my chest, fixing a distraught look on my face. "I'm so lost! I was at the ball, and I got completely turned around. Can you help me?"

He hesitated for a moment, looking confused. That was all the opening I needed. I stepped forward quickly to close the distance between us, pressing my lips to the shell of his ear and whispering promises of eternal happiness, fulfillment, and sinful pleasures. I was so amped up with adrenaline that the charm poured out of me, stronger than I'd ever felt it.

The guard's jaw slackened, and he leaned into me. "Yes... yes, I can help you."

"Good." I ran my fingers lightly down his chest. "I'm looking for a hallway on the fifth floor with green carpet and a large door at the end. Do you know where that is?"

"Yes..." He shook his head slowly, his brow wrinkling. "But that's a restricted area. No one but palace staff allowed without permission."

Fuck. I pressed my palm to his chest, murmuring in his ear, "But *you* gave me permission."

The guard's angular features cleared. "Oh. Right. Come this way."

He started off down the hall and I caught his elbow, maintaining contact between us as I stroked his arm.

"Well done, kitten."

The voice in my ear almost made me jump out of my skin. I'd forgotten Akio and Fen were still listening in through the communication charm.

"Thanks," I muttered. "So far, so good. Now I just need to get into the room and destroy the receiver. How long will this guy stay loopy without me continuing to charm him?"

"I could keep someone under the influence for hours without contact. You? Probably minutes."

I snorted. "Thanks for the vote of confidence."

"Just being realistic, kitten. Be careful." Akio's voice was soft.

We turned into a hallway where another guard was stationed, and I quickly pulled the dark-haired guard back. When we were safely hidden around the corner, I murmured in his ear, "Get rid of him. Don't let him see me."

He straightened, his eyes regaining some focus now that he had a task. Holding my breath, I pushed him around the corner, hoping I wasn't about to sabotage this entire operation. If he told his buddy I was here, I'd be screwed. I didn't think I could charm them both.

Low voices floated down the hall, and a moment later, the guard returned, slicking back his hair and smiling at me shyly like a love-struck little boy.

I peered around the corner.

The hallway was empty. Damn. Having an escort was amazing.

As the tall man led me through the enormous palace, I paid close attention to every turn we took, trying to memorize our route. This place was a maze.

Finally, he guided me down a small side hall, and our feet met with green carpet. My chest clenched with excitement. This was it. Now that I could see our destination, I took the lead, tugging the sluggish man toward the large cherry wood door at the end of the hall. The familiar glow of a ward pulsed faintly across the surface of the door.

"Open it," I commanded, trailing my hand down the side of his face. He shuddered with pleasure and I winced with disgust. I'd never get used to this charm magic. It felt so fucked up to have control over another person like this. But it worked. The man reached over, pressing his hand to a panel next to the door. The ward flickered and faded.

I pushed the heavy door open, eyes darting around the room. There was no one inside. A large table took up the middle of the room. Papers and maps were spread over the dark wood. More maps were displayed on the walls in between the large, arched windows, reminding me eerily of the war room at the Resistance headquarters. Except here, one wall held a giant glass display with dozens of small glowing cubes arranged neatly in rows. This was definitely the room Rat had seen. And those were definitely tracking spell receivers.

Leaving the guard holding the door open, I stepped into the room. There didn't appear to be any labels on the glowing receivers; whoever had set them up obviously had some other way of monitoring them. I ran my fingers over the smooth surface of one, wondering whether I'd feel any reaction if I touched the one that was connected to me. But I didn't have time to go through them all individually. And besides, destroying the entire display would set the Representatives further back on their heels.

Too bad there wasn't a quiet way to do it.

I backed away from the shelves, shooting a glance at the guard, who still stared vaguely into space. "Close the door."

He stepped into the room, letting the heavy wooden door shut behind him.

Raising my hand, I summoned an orange ball of fire like Jae had taught me. But this time, I kept feeding magic into it until it grew into a large orb a foot across. Then I hurled it across the room. It struck the glass shelves, and they exploded. Shards of glass rained down as the cubes crashed to the floor, breaking open. When they broke, the light inside them flared briefly, then flickered out.

A cold tingle ran down my arm to my fingertips, echoing the feeling I'd had when Rat placed the tracking spell on me.

Relief flooded my body. The spell was broken.

A few receivers remained intact on the floor, but I didn't want to risk another loud crash. So I stomped on them, putting my ridiculous heels to good use for once.

"What was that noise? Are you all right?" Akio's voice in my ear was colored with fear.

"It's done," I said. "The tracking receiver is broken. All of them are, actually."

"Yeah, they are! I knew you could do it!" Fenris crowed.

"Now get out of there, killer. Let's wrap this thing up and go home."

I wasn't sure if he was talking about the Resistance base or my little apartment, but either way, I heartily agreed with him.

Turning, I was about to head for the door when a small folder on the table caught my eye. A piece of paper stuck out of it, bearing the name *Christine O'Connell.*

Was that the same Christine I knew? I'd never gotten her last name. Shit. Did the Representatives know she was leading the Resistance? What else did they know about her?

There was no time to read through it now, but this was information the Resistance needed. I shoved the loose papers back inside the file folder and snatched up the whole thing.

"Hey... what are you...? You can't be back here." The guard shook his head, his sharp features contorting in a grimace as his eyes regained clarity. He stared in horror at the wreckage of glass and broken spells strewn across the floor. "*What did you do?*"

Dropping the folder, I yanked up my skirt, pulling out a dagger and whipping it at the guard. But before it could strike, light flared around his body. My dagger sailed ineffectually over the head of the panther that now crouched where the guard had stood. It hit the wood behind him with a dull *thunk* and quivered there.

"Well, fuck."

CHAPTER 25

THE PANTHER GROWLED, his lips pulling back from his sharp teeth as he sank back on his haunches, muscles coiled like springs.

"Killer, are you okay? What's wrong?" Fenris's panicked voice came in my ear.

"Got a little problem," I murmured, eyes glued to the big cat in front of me. "The guard slipped out of my charm. I'm trapped."

"Use your transport spell. Get out of there, kitten. Now." Akio's voice was tight.

"No!" I hissed. "If I bail, it'll leave Jae stranded. When the Representatives find out what happened, they'll pin the blame on him."

"He can handle it. Trust me, he would not want you to risk yourself for him."

For fuck's sake. When this was over, we were going to have to have a serious talk about who was allowed to sacrifice themselves for whom. But I didn't have time to argue about it now.

In one smooth movement, I pulled the transport spell Jae had given me from the bodice of my dress and threw it to the ground, raising my foot to stomp on it. A roar erupted as I brought my foot down, and heavy paws hit my shoulders, throwing me backward as the purple smoke billowed up from the transport spell—without me in it.

The smoke dissipated a moment later, leaving me stranded in the room with an angry panther shifter pinning me down. His jaws snapped, and I twisted out of the way, scrabbling desperately for the knife in my thigh sheath.

No. Use what you have. Use magic!

Baring my teeth, I pressed my hands to the fur of the panther's underbelly, summoning a burst of fire. The panther howled, leaping away. I scrambled to my feet, calling up the animal inside me.

My bones cracked and reformed, and a moment later, I crouched on the slick marble floor in wolf form.

The panther circled, his tail twitching angrily. An angry red blotch marred his stomach where my fire had burned off his black fur. I barely had time to register his movement before he leapt toward me again. I met him with snapping teeth, catching his ear as he bowled me over.

We skidded across the floor, crashing into the shards of glass from the destroyed shelves. I ripped my teeth away from the panther's ear, tasting blood. He swung a giant paw at me, hitting the side of my face so hard I saw stars.

I rolled away and stood, and the panther stalked toward

me, backing me into a corner. Heart pounding, I flicked my gaze to the door. It was locked, and I didn't think I had the strength to break through it, but there was no way I was shifting back to human form with this panther in the room. I cast around frantically for another escape route.

The window.

We were on the fifth floor, but the fourth floor extended out beyond this level, so it was only a single-story drop to the roof below us.

I lunged for the panther, snapping at his neck. He circled the other way, avoiding my strike, but I didn't care. As soon as I had an opening, I raced toward the window on the far side of the room, leaping through it.

The moment I broke the windowpane, an alarm split the air. The glass shattered, falling alongside me like glittering snowflakes as I plunged toward the roof below. The surface was flat and covered with a gray tar-like substance.

My paws thudded painfully against the hard roof and I stumbled, rolling out of the way just in time to avoid being crushed by the palace guard, who had jumped through after me. The moment he landed, I clamped my teeth hard around his front leg.

The panther yowled, his cry joining the keening shriek of the alarm rising in the air. He leapt on me, using his greater weight to pin me down as his jaws closed on my shoulder. Pain ripped through me. I thrashed and squirmed, trying to dislodge him, but he clung like a burr.

I could feel my energy flagging. I'd used more magic

tonight than I ever had before, and I wasn't used to fighting as a wolf.

Summoning all my strength, I pressed my back paws into the panther's belly and kicked. He growled as my nails scraped the tender flesh of his stomach, stumbling as he regained his feet. I turned tail and ran, racing along the flat roof toward the access door on the far side.

When the thudding steps of the panther behind me reached my sharp ears, I stopped suddenly, turning to face my pursuer. As he neared me, I clamped my teeth around his neck, using his forward momentum to hurl him over the side of the roof.

With a feline shriek, the panther's body sailed through the air and disappeared from view.

Panting heavily, I limped over to the edge of the roof and peered down. His still form was sprawled on the manicured ground below.

My stomach roiled.

If I hadn't killed him, he would've killed me. I knew that. But remembering what Fen had said about shifters being forced into the service of the Gifted, guilt twinged my heart.

This is why we're fighting. To end all this.

Backing away from the edge, I focused on the pain in my shoulder, letting healing magic flow through me to fill the break in the pattern of my life force. By the time my skin closed, it felt like I was pulling magic from the bottom of a very deep well. I was hanging onto the illusion spell around me by a thread.

The alarm was still blaring, alerting the entire palace to the break-in. I shifted quickly back to human form. I had a momentary flash of panic that I'd be naked—I'd spent several hours over the past few days practicing shifting, and it was still about fifty-fifty whether I had clothes when I shifted back —but my dress materialized with me, thank the gods.

No shoes though. And my attempt at an up-do was pretty much destroyed.

I hardly cared. Barefoot, I staggered toward the rooftop access door, pressing against it with all my weight. I could hear shouts from the fifth story room as I slipped through the door.

"The guard is dead. I'm heading back to the ballroom. Tell Christine the Resistance's location is safe," I muttered into my communication charm as I stepped quickly down the stairs.

Two stories down, I peered out of the stairwell. A pair of demon guards with dusky red skin ran by, and as soon as they disappeared around a corner, I darted into the hallway. I was nowhere near the route the guard had brought me down originally, but I headed in the direction I thought was north.

The magically amplified alarm had finally stopped screeching, but tension still hung in the air, filling the silence. Four Blighted men in tuxes rushed by, and I ducked to the side. They couldn't see me through the illusion, but they'd definitely notice me if they ran into me.

Their attire encouraged me. They must have come from the ballroom. I slipped down the same hallway they'd turned out of, and almost collapsed with relief when I recognized my surroundings. The ballroom waited at the end of this corridor.

Allowing my invisibility illusion to drop, I rushed down the hall and pulled the door open.

The room was in disarray. Women shrieked—although ironically, none as loud as when that waiter had spilled a drink on them—and men's voices rose angrily as the palace staff tried to calm everyone down. A quick glance at the front of the room revealed the large entrance doors closed off. They must not be letting anyone leave.

I scanned the space for Corin and Jae. My eyes lit on Jae first, the relief on his normally placid features so stark it was almost funny. I stepped toward him, but I hadn't made it far when a hand caught my wrist.

Turning, I looked up into a pair of narrowed brown eyes. The man peering down his nose at me was thin and lanky, with carefully coifed brown hair accented by twin streaks of gray at his temples. He had puffy bags under his eyes, and a scowl deepened the lines on his face.

"Just where do you think you're going?" he asked softly. His voice had a raspy quality, like he needed a glass of water.

"I—I got separated from my date in the chaos." I lowered my eyes demurely, hoping I didn't look as beat up as I felt. The blood soaking my fur had disappeared when I shifted from wolf to human form, so at least I wasn't that obvious.

"That's a staff door." The man's dark brown eyes narrowed. "And the head of security made it clear no one was to leave until we secured the palace grounds."

"I didn't know. I was—"

His grip on my wrist tightened, his magic surging. It didn't feel particularly strong, but his blue and red attire clearly identified him as a government official. So he wielded both magical and political power, neither of which I was in a position to fight right now.

"I haven't seen you before. Who did you come here with?" he demanded.

I swallowed. I was tempted to lie to protect Jae, but it wasn't a deception that would hold up for long, and it would make us both look guilty when the truth came out.

"Jae. Jae Nocturne. He's over—"

I started to point but realized it was completely unnecessary. Jae was already striding over, a muscle in his jaw ticking. Behind him, Corin was edging subtly through the crowd closer to us.

"What is the meaning of this?" Jae's voice was sharp and cold as ice. "Please unhand my friend right now."

The man scoffed. "Ah, Jonas's boy. She's *your* date? Well, son, I'm afraid I can't let her go until she explains what she was doing behind a private staff door after there was an attack on the palace."

"I told you, I got lost! I—"

"Really? And how exactly does one manage to lose their way in a single room? You were told to stay in the ballroom, which should have made getting lost quite impossible." The man's voice rose in volume as he spoke, drawing the attention of the people around us.

"I was frightened," I murmured, trying to sound contrite instead of angry. Who the fuck was this guy?

"I'm sorry, Rain." Jae's voice was low but firm. "We were separated in the confusion when the alarm sounded. She was probably looking for me. My friend is new to Denver and has never attended a palace function before. She didn't know the protocol. I would hate for her to think this is how the Representatives treat a powerful Gifted visitor."

The man—Rain—pushed me through the milling crowd toward the front of the room where Jae's father stood talking to a palace guard, keeping my wrist torqued uncomfortably behind my back. I could probably break his hold, but then what? We were surrounded by too much magical firepower to survive a fight.

Jae kept pace with us as I staggered along in front of Rain, his worried green eyes meeting mine.

"Chief Advisor Blackshear, I really must insist—" he tried again, but Rain cut him off.

"Don't imagine you can throw your father's rank around and get what you want, son," he hissed. "That would only work if I believed he'd back you up, and you and I both know that's not going to happen."

We were making enough of a spectacle to call attention, and Jonas Nocturne looked up as we approached, his cool, surprised eyes meeting mine. Shit. This was about to get so bad—not just for me, but for Jae. My chest rose and fell rapidly, and I dug my heels in, bare feet sliding on the marble as I pushed back against Rain, slowing our progress.

Suddenly, a clear, feminine voice cut through the noise of the room.

"Stop!"

CHAPTER 26

RAIN PULLED up short behind me, and I almost slipped as my leverage against him was suddenly met with no resistance. Regaining my balance, I glanced around the ballroom, searching for the source of the voice.

By now, we had the attention of the entire ballroom, and the crowd parted to make way for a small woman with a shock of short, white hair. Her lined face was kind, and her delicate features made me think she must have been stunning when she was young. She wore a deep blue and red dress in a conservative style, the fabric so luxurious it made her look like a queen.

And her eyes were locked on me.

The man holding me sighed, keeping his grip tight even as he turned in the old woman's direction. "What is it, Beatrice?"

Beatrice stopped a few feet away from me, her gray eyes regarding me intensely. Now that she was this close, I realized how petite she truly was. She couldn't have been taller than five feet.

Her wrinkled hands twisted together as she studied me.

"Child, where are you from?"

Shit. We'd never worked out any kind of back-story for me —for "Lana the Gifted," the high society member I was pretending to be. I shot a glance at Jae, and he nodded slightly. Which meant... what, exactly? I wished I had the ability to communicate with him telepathically, like I could with Fen when we were both in wolf form.

"I'm from Wyoming. I haven't been in Denver long," I answered finally, keeping my answer truthful but deliberately vague.

"Wyoming?" The woman's brow furrowed, and she clucked her tongue. "No. That doesn't...."

She stepped closer, lifting her hand to tilt my chin down. The backs of her knuckles swept down the curve of my cheek, and her light gray gaze flickered over my features as if she was searching for something in my face.

Rain shifted impatiently. "Beatrice, there's been a break-in, and we need to get to the bottom of it. We really don't have time to—"

"Lana?"

Beatrice's voice was little more than a whisper, but it was enough to shut Rain up and stop my heart.

How did she know my name?

I'd never seen her before in my life, and I could count on the fingers of a single hand the number of people in Denver who had known me by name before I fell in with the Resistance. And one of those people was a ghost.

This woman wasn't connected with the Resistance somehow, was she? Judging by the shocked looks on Jae and Corin's faces, no.

Instead of answering her, I just gaped wordlessly, mind churning. Beatrice frowned, pulling her hand back. She seemed to suddenly doubt herself and shook her head with a small laugh. "I'm sorry, child. I thought—"

"How do you know my name?" I finally found my voice, and Beatrice's gaze snapped up.

"I knew it! It *is* you!" A delighted smile spread across her face.

"How do you know me?" I insisted.

The woman's smile quavered as a tear slipped down her cheek.

"Child, I'm your grandmother."

"*What?*"

That outburst came from Rain, who scoffed skeptically while I struggled to find words. Or breathe. The woman's gray eyes shimmered with tears, but their similarity to my own was striking. My emotions ricocheted from joy to panic to anger, finally settling on disbelief. I hated to agree with that asshole Rain on anything, but how the hell could this woman know she was my grandmother? I'd never seen her before in my life.

Or maybe you just don't remember, a voice my mind interjected.

All my earliest memories were of the Blighted settlement

I'd grown up in on the plains of Wyoming, but that still left a good five or six years of my childhood unaccounted for. And thanks to the camp's old-timers, whose memories stretched back further than mine, I knew I hadn't been born at the Blighted settlement. I'd arrived there at some point as a small child.

"Beatrice, really." Rain stepped closer to her, lowering his voice. Oh, *now* he wanted to keep from making a spectacle? "We all lost loved ones to the Great Death. I'm aware that you miss your family, but you cannot bring them back to life with wishful thinking."

"I wouldn't dare to wish. I hadn't even dared to hope," Beatrice murmured, her voice shaking. "But it's her. Don't you see the resemblance?"

"What's going on here?" Jonas stepped into our small circle, glancing from Beatrice to Rain to me.

Rain's irritation was palpable as he fixed a burning glare on me. "Beatrice thinks this young woman is her long-lost granddaughter."

I expected Jae's father to have a similar reaction to Rain at this news, so his response startled me. Rather than scoffing, he seemed intrigued. His cool gaze flicked between me and Beatrice, more assessing this time.

"I do see the resemblance. And it would explain Ms. Crow's great power. Beatrice, do you have any proof of this?"

"No, just a... feeling," she admitted. "But a reader can tell us quickly enough."

"Before we get too deeply entrenched in this little family reunion, there's another issue that must be resolved." Rain scowled at me, his magic roiling. "I caught this woman slipping through a staff-only door mere minutes after the alarm went off."

Jonas hesitated, his intelligent green eyes gleaming.

"It was just a mix-up. I got lost!" I repeated my excuse, though it sounded more desperate and false every time I said it.

Rain snorted, but before he could say anything, a palace guard pushed open the door and hustled over to Jonas, speaking quickly and quietly in his ear. The Minister of Justice listened intently, then nodded.

"Clean it up," Jonas told the guard. "And interrogate the rest of the guards. Make sure he didn't have any accomplices." He shifted his attention to Rain. "Let her go."

"What? But I—"

"They've identified the perpetrator. A panther shifter posing as a palace guard. He broke into a room on the fifth floor and died attempting to escape. Perhaps you should worry more about properly vetting your staff than leveling accusations against relatives of our most distinguished Representatives." Jonas's voice was cold and measured.

This woman was a Representative?

My blood chilled, and I shot her a glance.

She didn't look anything like how I'd imagined the Gifted government leaders. She was too old and... *nice* looking. Her sweet face twisted with worry as she watched me.

With a huff, Rain finally released his grip on my wrist. I shook my hand out lightly, stepping away from him. I had the uncomfortable feeling I was being used as part of a power play between these two men, but fuck if I could figure out what game they were playing.

Jae stepped up next to me, resting a hand lightly on my waist, and the contact instantly soothed me. I had an impulse to lean into his touch, to shrink back into the protective shield of his embrace. It was a strange feeling. I'd never been the type to shy away from confrontation. Usually, I met it with open arms—and a dagger in each hand.

But though danger hung heavy in the air around us, I couldn't figure out exactly where the threat came from. No one brandished weapons or hurled fireballs. This was a battle of politics, and it was completely foreign to me. I caught Corin's eye. He stood in the crowd gathered around us, his face reflecting the confusion I felt.

"Are you all right, my dear?" Beatrice brushed past Rain, catching my hand.

"I'm fine." I forced a smile.

She shot a glare at Rain, and he wilted a bit under her ire. Drawing himself back up, he faced me, his eyes narrowing as he gazed at me intently. "I apologize, Ms. Crow. It was my mistake. You are, of course, most welcome in our palace."

"Crow?" Beatrice squeezed my hand. "No, darling. If I'm right—and I grow more certain with every passing moment that I am—you're not a Crow. You're a Lockwood."

THE READER WAS A PLUMP, middle-aged woman with soft fingers. They felt like little balls of dough between my fingers as she held one of my hands in hers, her other hand grasping Beatrice's.

We sat in a small chamber one floor above the ballroom. After Rain's apology, he'd hustled us swiftly out of the room, apparently no longer so keen to have this scene play out in front of an audience now that it involved his humiliation. Jonas had stepped away to consult with the palace guards. It didn't escape my notice that he hadn't once acknowledged Jae during the exchange in the ballroom.

As we trekked up the stairs, I tried to think of a subtle way to tell Akio and Fen what was happening, but I couldn't risk revealing the communication charm I was wearing, and talking to myself aloud would definitely look suspicious. Hopefully they'd picked up enough of the conversation to understand the gist of this new development.

Beatrice insisted Jae be allowed to come with me, but Corin had been left behind, maintaining his cover as one of the Blighted staff. I prayed he'd be able to slip out through the kitchens the same way he came in.

Small noises fell from the reader's parted lips, and her eyelids fluttered. The heat of Rain's stare tickled the back of my neck as we all waited for the woman to hand down her verdict.

Finally, the white film over her eyes faded, and she blinked.

"Well, your pattern of magic is very similar. I would say you're almost certainly blood relatives."

"Ah. Praise the gods," Beatrice breathed.

"Although," the reader added, turning to me, "yours is quite a bit stronger, and a bit… strange." Her gaze flicked to Jae, and I wondered if she could sense the connection between us like Asprix had. Could she also tell my magic was attached to three other people?

I'd been nervous about sitting down with the Representatives' reader, afraid she'd somehow be able to see right down into my soul and find out all the truths I was trying to keep hidden. But of course, that was beyond her power. Readers could interpret the shape and feel of magic, but they couldn't decipher thoughts.

"Well." Rain cleared his throat. "That answers that. Welcome to Denver, Ms. *Lockwood*." His voice twisted on the last word, as if it pained him to say it.

Beatrice turned in her seat, her gray eyes bright as she regarded me. "You said you're new to Denver?"

I nodded, keeping my gaze steady.

Guess that's the story we're going with.

"Then you must come live with me! Goodness, I have a house that's too big for an army, let alone one person. And there's so much I need to know. Where did you…? How did you…?" She stopped and patted at her flushed cheeks, tears glistening in her eyes again. "Darling Lana. We've lost so much time. I don't know what happened to you, but I want to find out everything. Sweet girl, I've missed you so much."

A lump rose in my throat, and I had the strangest urge to reach over and hug her. Although I'd made my own family in the Wyoming encampment—Margie and Corin had been all I needed—here was a woman who was my actual flesh and blood.

But she was Gifted.

A Representative.

I swallowed, the lump in my throat turning to shards of glass. I didn't know this woman at all. And I wasn't sure I wanted to.

"Killer?" Fenris murmured softly in my ear, his tone tender. "We updated Christine on what's happening. She wants you to accept your grandmother's offer. We have a chance to infiltrate the highest levels of government, and we have to take it."

His deep voice soothed my racing heart, even as his words sent my mind spinning.

Christine was right. All we'd intended to do on this mission was keep the Resistance's location safe, but this strange new development was a gift to the entire rebellion. We could anticipate the Representatives' moves against us, sew discord in their ranks, and lay the groundwork for an uprising.

If I could play my part.

Beatrice watched me with anxious eyes, hanging onto my answer like her life depended on it.

I took a deep breath, reaching up to clasp Jae's hand on my shoulder.

"Thank you, Beatrice. I'd love that."

CHAPTER 27

THE PEELING PAINT, stained wood floor, and grungy walls of my apartment had never looked better. The ancient, buzzing fridge had never seemed more precious. Even my ghost "roommate" who kept the TV on too loud at all hours of the day and night suddenly seemed like the best companion a girl could have.

I never would've thought I'd miss this place when I finally got a chance to leave, but now I found myself lingering, unable to say goodbye to the shitty apartment that had been my tiny haven in the Outskirts for the past eight years.

"You're sure that's all you want to bring?" Fen asked again, eyeing the small worn bag I'd packed with the essentials—clothes, my favorite book, and every weapon I owned.

"Yeah. Beatrice thinks I just moved here, so it wouldn't make sense for me to have more stuff than this. Besides, what am I gonna do? Bring my furniture? My mugs? A spatula? I'm sure anything I own, she has a better, fancier version."

I couldn't keep the bitterness out of my voice. I understood the reasoning behind Christine's decision to send me into the Capital undercover, but that didn't mean I was excited about it. It was one thing to find out I had magical abilities, but something else entirely to be forced to adopt the lifestyle of the Gifted. I could almost feel the corruption, entitlement, and bigotry coating me like a slimy film, and I hadn't even gotten to Beatrice's mansion yet.

Despite their sentimental value, I'd get by just fine without my crappy kitchen supplies and beat up furnishings. The only thing I truly regretted leaving behind was my prize bookshelf full of books. But....

I turned to Akio, who lounged against the wall by the bedroom door. Less-than-shockingly, the incubus had somehow forgotten to put a shirt on again this morning. The twisted, intricate designs of black ink covering his sculpted arms and chest pulled my gaze, but I managed to keep my eyes focused on his face.

"Hey, Akio... um, do you want my books? You had so many before your house got wrecked. I know my collection isn't as big as yours was, but it's a start. You can add to it."

He blinked, pushing away from the wall in a fluid movement. The expression on his face was different than any I'd ever seen him wear. He almost looked... moved.

Akio stalked toward me like a cat, his eyes fixed on mine. My heart pounded faster with every step he took, the intensity of his gaze rooting me to the spot. For some reason, my fight-or-flight instinct kicked in. The demon put me so off balance, the warring attraction and antipathy between us making it hard to feel certain of anything in his presence.

When he reached me, his large hand swept around the back of my neck, cradling my head.

"I'd be honored, kitten. Thank you."

Akio bent his head to press a kiss to my cheek. The contact of his skin against mine, the warmth of his breath tickling my ear, and the softness of his lips sent a spark of fire shooting through my body. He lingered there for a moment, and I locked my knees, trying not to reveal how much he affected me.

When he finally drew back, his pupils were dilated, making his eyes look even darker and more enigmatic than usual. He strolled over to my bookshelf, running a finger over the spines of the books. Somehow, that small gesture made me shiver, as if it was my skin he caressed instead of the paper bindings.

"This is an excellent collection. You have good taste," he murmured, and my chest swelled. "Although there is room for improvement."

I rolled my eyes, almost grateful for his snarky comment. Annoyance helped dispel the unsettling dreamy feelings his incubus charm gave me.

"We should get going soon," Jae said, glancing around the room. He had offered to drive me to Beatrice's home, since it would hardly do for me to arrive in my beat up green Honda. It wouldn't be *proper*.

Suppressing a grimace, I nodded, hefting my bag over my

shoulder. I only held it there for two seconds before Corin snatched it from my grip to carry it for me. I would've argued, but I knew he needed to do something to feel useful. The upcoming separation was wearing on all of us, Corin most of all.

After Jae and I had finally escaped the People's Palace, we'd rendezvoused with Akio and Fen near a park a few blocks from the palace grounds. We'd waited nervously for several hours, and I'd been about ready to storm the palace by force when Corin finally appeared. Maeve, the Resistance member working in the kitchens, had been able to sneak him out.

That was two days ago, and we'd spent the intervening time at my apartment. We didn't dare go back to the Resistance headquarters; we'd just secured the location by destroying the tracking spell and didn't want to risk another exposure. But Christine had been in touch by phone, and we'd devoted many hours to discussing my undercover operation. The Resistance leader seemed to have decided to trust me for now. Or at least, to use me, which worked out pretty much the same in the end.

"I can't believe you're leaving," Ivy said sadly, her translucent features crumpling in a girlish pout. Part of me wondered if she'd even remember I was gone once her favorite TV show came on, but I kept that to myself.

"Yeah, me neither." I cleared my throat. "I'll miss you, Ivy."

"You doing okay, killer?" Fenris ran his hand down my arm, lacing his fingers with mine and raising our joined hands to his lips.

I nodded, not trusting my voice. When I was sure I could speak without crying, I said, "You guys know this doesn't count as leaving you, right? I'm only going because Christine wants me to, because the Resistance *needs* me to. I don't want to go."

"We know, Lana." Jae squeezed my shoulder.

"And we'll be with you, as much as we can be. You've got a phone and your communication charm. If you need anything, say the word and we'll be there." Corin's eyes blazed with determination and worry.

"Thanks, guys. I'll try to reserve my emergency calls for actual emergencies and not just 'I hate this so much; get me the fuck out of here' freak-outs."

"Hey," Corin interjected seriously. "*Anything.*"

My heart warmed, and I rubbed the back of my neck. "I just don't know what to expect. I can't figure Beatrice out. She's Gifted, and one of the highest-ranking members of the government, apparently. But she seems so... sweet." I shot Corin a glance. "She reminds me of Margie a little bit, actually."

Saying that out loud almost felt like a betrayal of the gentle, intelligent woman who had served as a stand-in mother to me and Corin in our younger years, and I was relieved when Corin nodded.

"Yeah, same here."

"But how can she be, if she lives and abides by this system? There's nothing *sweet* about how the Gifted treat the Blighted —or even the Touched, for that matter." I shifted my gaze to

Fen, who raised his eyebrows in agreement and kissed my hand again, nipping the skin with his teeth this time. A flush crept up my cheeks, but I didn't pull my hand away.

"I don't know, Lana." Corin tipped his head, his blue eyes warm. "But that's why you're going. To get answers."

I squared my shoulders. "You're right. I can do this. I have to." I turned to Jae. "Ready whenever you are."

Only one person was needed to drive me to the Capital, but each of my four had insisted on coming. After I locked the apartment door and solemnly handed the keys to Corin, we all trooped downstairs to Jae's car. Without even asking, I clambered into the middle seat. It might have felt awkward that first day we met, but today, the feel of being pressed between Akio and Fenris was exactly the kind of grounding I needed.

We drove in silence, passing through the wide gate in the wall around the Capital. As the gate swung shut behind us, I twisted in my seat, a sudden burst of panic flaring at the feeling that I might never see the Outskirts again.

Fenris kissed my hair, burying his nose in my locks and inhaling my scent. The sensation tickled my scalp, and I squirmed slightly.

"You've got this, killer."

His whispered words buoyed my spirits—until Jae pulled to a stop outside a lavish, gated stone mansion. The gate swung open as we approached, and he pulled through, stopping at the entrance to the circular drive. I tried not to gape at the huge fountain in the middle, where sunlight glittered on large drops of water enchanted to leap from the pool in the shape of fish.

"Holy gods," Corin breathed, a combination of awe and disgust in his voice. Beatrice hadn't been kidding. She could put up a small army in that house.

That mansion.

That castle.

Three stories tall and sprawling wide into separate wings, it was impeccably kept, the pale stone unnaturally spotless. Grand white columns rose high in front of the dark cherry wood door. The hedges were neatly trimmed, and glittering fairy lights sparkled in the trees.

I was supposed to live *here?*

"We can't stay. Until we know more about your grandmother, it's better she doesn't know too much about us," Jae said, pulling my attention back to the interior of the car.

"I know. Stay safe, okay?"

"You too. Stay in contact. Please." His voice was rough.

Fenris reluctantly got out and turned to help me exit the car. Corin handed me my bag before Fen slipped back inside.

For a moment, I stood staring through the windows into the sleek silver car, which seemed to hold all the pieces of my heart. Jae seemed similarly frozen, sitting stock-still with his hand on the wheel as he, Corin, Akio, and Fen gazed at me.

Then he blinked, breaking the spell, and the car rolled slowly around the drive and through the gate. It swung shut behind them, and I hefted my bag higher on my shoulder, taking a deep breath as the soft *plop, plop* of water droplets plunking into the fountain filled the sudden silence.

The mansion loomed before me, perfectly framed by the white-capped mountains rising behind it.

Beautiful.

And terrifying.

THANK YOU FOR READING!

I hope you enjoyed reading *Bound by Magic* as much as I loved writing it. And don't worry, there's more coming!

Lana and her men's adventure will continue in *Game of Lies*, book two of the *Magic Awakened* trilogy.

She knows how to handle herself in a fight. But navigating a palace full of scheming Gifted politicians will be a challenge unlike any she's ever faced...

In the meantime, you can keep reading with a free copy of *Kissed by Shadows*, a prequel novella that has more of Corin and Lana's backstory.

Sign up for my reader newsletter at https://www. sadiemossauthor.com/subscribe, and I'll send you your free copy!

MESSAGE TO THE READER

PLEASE CONSIDER LEAVING A REVIEW! Honest reviews help indie authors like me connect with more awesome readers like you. It is truly one of the best ways you can help support an author whose work you enjoy!

If you liked this book, I would be forever grateful if you'd take a minute to leave review (it can be as short or long as you like) on my book's Amazon page.

Thank you so much!

ACKNOWLEDGMENTS

First and foremost, thank you to my incredible husband and my sweet puppy for putting up with all of my mad ramblings about the *Magic Awakened* series.

Thank you, Jacqueline Sweet, for the amazing cover! You really brought Lana to life.

To my amazing beta readers: thank you, thank you, thank you!

ABOUT THE AUTHOR

Sadie Moss is obsessed with books, craft beer, and the supernatural. She has often been accused of living in a world of her own imagination, so she decided to put those worlds into books.

When Sadie isn't working on her next novel, she loves spending spending time with her adorable puppy, binge-watching comedies on Hulu, and hanging out with her family.

She loves to hear from her readers, so feel free to say hello at sadiemoss.author@gmail.com.

And you want to keep up with her latest news and happenings, you can like her Facebook page, or follow her on Twitter, Goodreads, and Amazon.

Made in the USA
Coppell, TX
23 June 2020